"Put him on the table."

He felt himself being hoisted onto a hospital table.

"You got some cuffs?" the deputy asked. "We gonna have to take our manacles with us. We use them a lot on niggers back in Briarville."

"Roll up his sleeve."

The deputies turned him onto his side so that he was facing a wall covered with thick padding.

Padded cell, he thought, surprised that such rooms actually existed outside of movies.

"What you got there, doc?"

"Just something to keep him quiet…. He'll be able to think but he won't be able to talk or move."

"They ought to feed that stuff to every nigger in the South," a deputy snorted.

Other Holloway House Originals by Joseph Nazel

EVERY GOODBYE AIN'T GONE

Joseph Nazel

An Original Holloway House Edition
HOLLOWAY HOUSE PUBLISHING COMPANY
LOS ANGELES, CALIFORNIA

Published by
HOLLOWAY HOUSE PUBLISHING COMPANY
8060 Melrose Avenue, Los Angeles, California 90046

International Standard Book Number 0-87067-764-0
Printed in the United States of America

Cover photograph by Jeffrey. Posed by professional models.
Cover design by Greg Salman.

EVERY GOODBYE
AIN'T GONE

AN OPEN LETTER

My Fellow Americans:

I'm a defiant motherfucker. I defy because I'm here and am going to *be* here. I'm a defiant motherfucker! And bold, and tired, but still bold and bad enough to tell you that I don't give a damn about how you feel or react to my defiance or my language; I don't care that what I say or might say might damage your plastic bubbles of self-righteous superiority.

I'm a defiant motherfucker!

I have to be; I've found, if I'm going to snap the lock on the golden girdles you wear around your minds, or shit-can the precious rules you have manufactured to hand-stroke your mounting perversions.

9

Yes, my fellow Americans, for once in this long-ass foot race that's kept me puffing, I don't give a damn about anything but the truth, which means, quite frankly, I no longer recognize phony sensibilities.

I'm going to stand here, black-ass bare and bold, and trip off on my wild-eyed, calming, soothing, satisfying, life-giving defiance. I'm going to grow fat on my rage. I'm going to finger-fuck the Statue of Liberty, Queen of Whores, until she begs..., drops to her knees, puts out her torch, and begs like a nigger for his life during lynching season, for that pussy-whipping that I am not about to dish out.

That's right, I've unconditioned myself from the clever conditioning that has drugged my mind, blinded me, fucked with my movements. I don't dig on or fantasize about chasing white skirts anymore. I don't get off when you find time to give credence to my existence by recognizing it.

Close your eyes and ears to what I'm putting down. Do it now before the shit gets deeper and, baby, let me tell you, it's gonna get just that—deeper, thicker, stickier, stinkier than rotting corpses. It's shit-or-get-off-the-pot time..., do you hear the first grrrrrrruuuuuuunt?!!!

I've been eating shit since day one.

I've been taking your shit.

I've been digging trenches for your shit.

I've been cleaning up after your shit.

I've been shit on.

I've been shit at.

I've walked in shit.

I've wallowed in shit (and acted like I liked it).

I've been thrown in shit (and grinned about it).

I've made my nest in shit (and paid more rent for it).

I've had the shit kicked out of me when I complained about the amount of shit that was coming my way…, uppity nigger that I am.

But it's coming back. It's turnaround time. Yes. It's coming back. Praise the Lawd and pass the toilet paper because it's coming back at you in a record breaking deluge *of shit!*

All that shit that's been steaming in me is going to come cascading down like a roaring waterfall and the only thing you can do about it is close your eyes, ears, and mouths…, stuff your noses with cotton or toilet paper, and lie back and take the weight because it's gonna get you! It's gonna smother you! It's gonna bury you! Large turds. Small turds. Squishy turds. Liquid turds.

Dig it! I'm going to enjoy every second of this release. I'm going to dig getting all this shit off my stomach, where its lain for so long fuckin' with my insides.

Yeah, I'm gonna dig every rhythmic grunt as the shit oozes out…, first in dribbles, then pellets, then missile-size bombs. Constipation time is over.

Yeah, I'm gonna pop my fingers and read Malcolm, Fanon, Dick Wright, and Baraka while in the porcelain library, where the bare bulb is going to jump to each thunderous grunt.

Oooooh yeah, it's gonna feel good whether you want to believe it or not and it's gonna be good for you!

There'll be no tambourine-slappin', amenin', hand shakin', peace talks, concessions, understandin' allowed during this ceremony.

Yeah, I'm gonna read Ex-Lax for my constipation, break wind, and the barrage is gonna begin. The shit is going to flood the streets and alleyways of your crisp white neighborhoods like murky water from a busted dam.

The shit is going to burn its way through the heart of sanctimonious America like a scorching lava from a too-long-dormant volcano,

Yeah! Volcano, that's what I am, have been but ain't been acting like. A volcano spits fire! A volcano vomits up death and destruction from the asshole of the earth.

It's not going to be a teaspoonful of shit that you can chase down with two or three dry martinis or wipe away with a crisp hundred-dollar bill, or bury in a potter's field or hide away in the slammers, or squish underfoot or apologize for and ignore.

Naw! This shit is going to come down on you in shovelsful, bucketsful, tubsful! Everywhere you turn there's going to be shit and more shit and more shit, settling on your marbled floors, seeping into your plush carpets, fouling your swimming pools, clogging your garbage disposals and toilet bowls, altering the courses of your rivers.

Pray, if you can remember how, if you think God

is still listening to you. Practice your breaststroke. Buy canoes, shovels, heavy digging machinery. But keep in mind that there aren't going to be any dark people, black, brown, or otherwise, who are going to volunteer to shovel shit for you. They're all going to be too busy shoveling the shit *to* you!

Are you still with me? Are you still picking up on what I'm putting down? Are you mesmerized by the rainbow of shit that is clouding your horizons? Have you decided to run for your lives or have you decided it's time to change your program?

But there's no place to run to, *baaby.* There's no place to hide—that I haven't already tried to hide in.

Face it! It's time! That time when up is down, and down is soaring out there, laughing, farting, and shitting up stuff that's been bottled up too long.

It's *the* time. That time when the fear of exploding from an overload of hand-me-down shit is stronger than any fears yet experienced.

Face it, and grow! But first, here's a little piss to christen the ground.

Sincerely Yours,

Rabbit

ONE

BORN AGAIN

He perched on the edge of his seat, ready for light, his eyes frozen on the postcard landscapes flashing by the window of the train. It was his first train trip in almost ten years and a giddy uneasiness drummed over his tingling flesh like the fingers of nervous hands.

The orange and crimson sunset quickly dissolved into the inky darkness that swallowed up the lush green tangle of the Deep South. And the darkness whizzed by in a numbing sameness beyond the window of the rocking train, the monotony broken only by the sudden appearances of beads of light floating in the murk like low-orbiting stars.

He clutched his release papers in the palm of a sweaty hand, ready to be presented on demand to anyone who might challenge his freedom, or worse yet his *sanity*. His freedom was something he had fought for, his sanity something he treasured and battled to preserve. Yet he had lost them both, or so he had been told and encouraged to believe by his keepers, who had tagged him to run a briar patch gauntlet by labeling him dangerously paranoid and mentally deranged. And during the early years of his confinement he was forced to play audience to doctors who traced over the years of his life, running rough fingers over his still-forming features, his private parts, his unhealed wounds. Blind men and women, they probed, poked, prodded, and eventually pigeonholed him, their prewritten definitions explaining even their contradictory findings.

"They" tagged him and defined his actions and attitudes, his life, past, present, *and future*. He hated them for their pomposity, their arrogance in thinking they could sketch a road map for his life. He hated himself for his vulnerability, for doing little more than defying them by continued existence, and a stubborn reclusiveness that they identified as symptomatic of his mental illness.

When "they" released him, he had been pronounced *cured* of the distortions in perception that prompted his confinement. Still, he fought them and insisted he had been little more than a political prisoner, confined because his attitudes did not conform to the insanity that passsed as the norm. They accepted his rantings as simply the side-effects of his long confinement; and they released him with the warning that "the world has changed, is changing, and will continue to change at its own pace." They cautioned that it would be to his benefit to find a place in that world rather than try to change it to fit his own calloused outlook.

He stared into the darkness engulfing the train and slipped under the spell of the rhythmic clack and clatter of wheels against rails. "Going home! Going home! Going home!" he muttered under his breath to the rhythm of the train. And framed in the window his image aped him in glassy silence with each *Going home! Going home! Going home!*

The train moved westward and the Deep South peeled away like a spent skin with each lurch of the train. And the constrictive closeness of Limbo, the State Asylum for the Mentally Ill, where he had weathered ten winters of enforced hibernation, eased somewhat. Tentatively he stretched his arms out from his sides, his release papers crushed in his right hand, and unfolded from the cramped position he had held since boarding the train.

Maybe the South *had* changed and the barriers to free movement and expression supposedly dissolved by the powers of the United States Supreme Court; still, hampered by brutal memories, he was not prepared as yet to test the freedoms of the "New South," where equality was no longer a dream but a reality—or so he had been told since his confinement. He somehow had become entombed in a world of dinosaurs, ancient monsters that no longer roamed the earth, they said, and he struggled not to believe them, though a show of belief might have shortened his period of confinement.

The darkness rushed by in a blur of speckled flashes that gave no definition to the dark shadows springing from the formless landscape. He pressed his back against the back of the seat, breathed deeply, and closed his eyes against the soft glow of the interior lights of the rocking train. The car was nearly empty of passengers. He felt unfortunate, unwilling to extend himself to "outsiders" until he was more certain of himself, his sanity, and the rhythm of the world surging around him like tides controlled by a fickle moon.

Mesmerized by the rolling rhythm of the train, he drifted back, pushed aside the veil of time that separated present from past, and memories assaulted him like angry bats screeching from the bowels of a dank cave. He shuddered slightly, pressed his eyelids tightly together until the pain throbbed at his temples. And he remembered how he came to be in the Deep South, his train ride through the "cotton curtain" and into the madness of a world fixated by color, or the lack of it, and he faced the memory because he knew his sanity would depend on the acceptance of failure.

It was summer, he remembered, and evening had brought little relief from the oppressive heat and humidity. He was riding in a Jim Crow car on the L&N Railroad line servicing the southern states. The coach was almost empty.

A smallish woman, her leathery skin a sickly yellow under the glow of the ceiling lights that ran the length of the coach, sat directly across the aisle from him, squatting in the center of the green leather bench seat, her belongings sprawled at her sides, effectively barring unwelcome intrusion though surrounded by empty seats. She stared straight ahead, though he occasionally sensed her eyes on him.

A silent trio huddled in the back of the coach, and he found that if he craned his head slightly and glared into the smudged window of the train he could see a glassy reflection of a woman and two small children. He turned in his seat and stared back at them. The woman seemed in her middle or late thirties, yet there was something in her face, like a single glowing ember in a pile of cold ashes, that suggested she might be much younger. There was something in her eyes, present even in the glassy image that mirrored her, that troubled him. He had seen it before, in the eyes of escapees from the South, who were rechristened "country" by those who did not understand. He had thought it to be fear, uncertainty, even cowardice, combined with a childlike innocence about life, founded in a lack of education and exposure. He would grow to learn the complex nature of conditions in the South and the terrible impact on its people. But then he could only feel a nagging sadness for the little boy who sucked lazily at the well-gnawed chicken bone until his mother took it from him, wiped his mouth with a piece of tissue, and dropped the bone in an open shoe box that rested on her lap.

Maybe, he thought, the boy would not grow up with the same beaten, hollow look he saw in the eyes of the boy's mother. He wanted to protect them, the mother and son, and the little girl, the color of roasting chestnuts, who slumbered fitfully in the crook of her mother's arm. He wanted to save them from their fears. But that was before he recognized he was being controlled by his own fears.

The train lurched and he found that he had to piss. The punishing rocking of the train jolted him, and the nagging monotony of the swishing fans at either end of the coach, stirring the thick, musty air, grated on his raw nerve endings. *He had to piss!* But he couldn't move. He knew that in order to satisfy a very natural urge he would have to become party to a very unnatural outlook and acknowledge and accept the existence of *white* plumbing and *Negro* plumbing.

Think about something else! he told himself as the pressure at his bladder increased with each passing second. He shifted on his seat, his pants clinging to his sweaty flesh. *Think about something else!* He pressed his knees tightly together. *Think about something else!*

He had thought to make a statement. He had come south to help in the struggle for freedom and justice and equality. Where was the justice? Shouldn't he stand and exercise his right to piss without regard to race, color, or creed? If he was to be the liberator, his duty was to walk down the aisle and *piss in whitey's head.*

For a long moment he had perched on the edge of the green leather bench poised between action and inaction, ignoring the icy rivers of sweat that drenched his clothing and turned to steam in the hot closeness of the coach, steam like a hot breath at the nape of his neck, sizzling upwards around his ears, forcing a hot mist before his eyes.

Yeah! he thought. He could do it. He would do it! And he pictured himself displaying an outrageous niggerness by strolling calmly down the aisle and not only pissing but shitting into the white-only plumbing. He had wanted to do it. But there was the blue-veined woman with the pale yellow skin, her eyes taking in everything and nothing, seeing only as she had been taught to see. And he wondered why she was riding in the Jim Crow car, wanting to ask her if she was some kind of nigger-lover. Or maybe she shared a "skinship" with him not visible in the dim light. What would she think?

And the woman behind him, reflected in the smudged pane, her travel-weary pickaninnies smothered under her wings like chicks under a black hen. He felt he could smell the stale, greasy chicken on their breaths. What would they think?

He started to move, his palms sticky with sweat. He rubbed the tips of his nervous fingers against the moist skin of his hands and rocked on the edge of his seat. Soon he would have to move or be shamed by his inaction.

His head was alive with the sound of the racing

train. His body caught the jerky, rocking, rolling, metallic lunge of the train, and he found himself clicking his tongue against the roof of his dry mouth in time to the clacking of the wheels along the steel ribbons uniting the South.

The train lurched into a tight curve as he stood to make what had become an urgent move. Pitched sideways into the aisle by the violent swaying of the train, he was slammed against the seats on the opposite side of the aisle. He scrambled to his feet, eyes wide, a warm trickle touching his inner thigh. The coach rocked heavily in the wrong direction and threw him backwards onto the woman with the pale yellow skin and the bulging veins, and her belongings were scattered onto the floor.

She screamed, "Git up from me! Git up from me!" in a thick southern drawl.

"I'm t-trying, lady," he countered, his hands searching for something solid.

"You're *touching* me!" she screamed. "Nigger, git off of me and quit *touching* me!"

There was no "skinship" between them. He bolted up from the seat as if snakebit and hoped the effort did not affect the delicate control he had over his swollen bladder.

"I wasn't touching you," he babbled. "I wasn't touching you!"

"You *touched* me!" she charged, her eyes milky white caps that caught the light and flashed angrily. She scrunched back against the far side of the seat and indicted him with a bony finger. "Nigger, you touched a white woman!"

"I wha…?" The objection clogged in his throat. He would have apologized, gathered up her belongings, and thought nothing else of it but her indictment froze him in his aisle. He had been charged with violating the longest-standing and most violently enforced taboo in the South. He had put his *black hands* on a white *woman!* Even without a guidebook on the ins and outs of being a man of color in the South he *knew,* without any doubt, that it mattered little that he hadn't intentionally touched the pale yellow woman with the blue-green veins that bulged now like wriggling snakes under her skin. It mattered little that the woman wasn't worth touching. He had been charged with the heinous crime, and for all intents and biological purposes the woman was probably white under her yellow skin. At least she said "nigger" as if she had been white a very *long* time.

Long moments tramped by, perspiration blinded him, and he still had to piss, *badly.* He pressed his knees tightly together and braced himself in the rolling, surging aisle by gripping the seat behind him with a trembling hand. He moved his lips but words did not come. He could think only of faded black-and-white photos he had seen in history books that never reached classrooms—photos of men, women, and children, poised, proud, and white, chests swollen by a perverted sense of purpose as they posed near the charred remains of someone who had violated a social taboo.

He was scared. "Lady, it was the train," he babbled. "It was the train! You know. I was just going to take a…, I mean, I had to go wash my hands, you know. The train. It was the train."

"You touched a white *woman*!" the bony finger indicted.

"I wasn't *trying* to touch you," he gasped. "Honest. I wouldn't touch you for anything." He looked away for help. Had he offended her by suggesting that she wasn't worth touching? Didn't they believe that black men spent every waking moment scheming up ways of *touching* a white woman and living to tell the tale? But the most pressing question was: would he live long enough to forget it ever happened?

"If a white man saw what you did he'd hang you up and skin you like a big hog," she spat.

And he thought, *The old bitch doesn't have any teeth* but said, "Honestly, madam," his voice tremoring in his throat, "I was really nothing more or less than a victim of the most unfortunate circumstances. You see," his grip on the supportive seat behind him slipped and his body swayed towards the old woman, who drew her legs defensively against her chest, "I…I was just trying to go to the washroom and wash my hands. It was simply an unfortunate accident caused by the…."

"You one of them educated niggers, ain'tcha?" she asked. Without waiting for an answer, she said, "You think you as good as white folks, don'tcha? Ain't even from 'round here, are you? You ain't one

26

of *our niggers!*"

He wanted to thank her for recognizing that he was somehow different from *her niggers*. But he could not help but feel he had a better chance of surviving the experience if he *was* one of *her* niggers, schooled in the fine art of *saving one's ass*. He reestablished his grip on the seat, and a pained expression twisted his face each time the train jolted and sent shock waves up his legs to tickle his bladder.

"You awright, *boy*?" the old woman asked. "You look funny. You sick or something?"

"I…ah was just trying to get to the washroom," he hissed through clenched teeth. "I would be more than happy to help you gather up your things."

"Boy!" she snapped violently, defending her nest like a spooked sparrow. "Don't you touch not none of my things if you sick with something!"

"No, madam," he objected, and a warm drop tingled against his flesh. He pressed his knees more tightly together. "I am not sick!" He was immediately sorry for the effort. The drop became a steady trickle tracing its way down his leg.

"*Boy,*" she said, her mouth like the spout of a volcano, the word a burst of scorching lava. "I don't know if you from the North or from somewheres out west where you niggers is allowed to do just like you want to…."

"Madam," he cut in, afraid to answer nature's call until released from her milky glare, "You see I've got to…."

"I'm talkin' to you, boy," she said sourly. "That's what you better learn first if you don't want to get taught the hard way. When white folks is talkin' to you, you listen. And don't be answering nothing you ain't been asked. You in the *South,* boy. Things ain't like they is where you come from, and if you want to git back there with your neck the same length it is now, you'd best listen!"

A lecture is better than a lynching, he tried to tell himself, but the pressure at his bladder had become an obsessive presence.

"Yes, ma'am," he muttered, his pained look a plea that was quickly misinterpreted.

"Boy, you *is* sick," the old woman said evenly and her lips fluttered in a tiny smile like the wings of a pale moth. "Why didn't you say you was sick? That's why you can barely stand up on your own two feet."

Was she glad that he was sick instead of aggressively social? Maybe it eased her burden of responsibility as well as his. Maybe she wasn't in the mood to knit at a lynching that night. "Yes, ma'am," he muttered dutifully, his shoulders hunched slightly forward. He fidgeted and the stinging trickle threatened to become a flood.

"Well, you remember everything I told you," she said, her voice somehow motherly.

"Yes, ma'am," he nodded and released his grip on the seat. He held his breath and started to back down the aisle towards the huddled trio, and hopefully a washroom. At the moment he had lost all urge to challenge the South's segregated plumbing. *He just had to piss.*

"You here visiting your folks?" she asked, and her eyes went opaque like dried drops of milk.

"No…, I mean, yes, ma'am. Grandma and grandpa, you know," he said and waddled backwards away from the cold stare. "Just visiting, you know." He rocked his head slightly on his trembling neck. "Got a little sick, you know, a little weak. Just gonna go back here and take my medicine."

"You take care and watch how you do down here," she warned, "and you have a nice time with your folks."

It was happening to someone else, he told himself. Not him! The whole thing was a scene out of the *Twilight Zone*, set up by a *Candid Camera* crew. It was crazy. And there he was, piss running down his leg and soaking into his sock, bowing and scraping to a toothless old woman with pale yellow skin, who had the power over his life and death, at least on that train. *He* was crazy.

When he reached the back of the train, where the woman sat with her two children, he paused. His hands held between his legs, knees drawn up, he poised on the tips of his toes. She stared up at him from her hollow eyes, and her lips moved in a knowing smirk. He forced a sheepish grin, backed out of the coach, and waddled in search of a washroom like a woman in a too-tight skirt. He found a door marked "Negro Only," tried the handle—too late.

The dam broke and a wild, scorching river rushed down his leg and into his shoe. Relief smothered shame for a moment and then his face burned as he understood that he could not return to the company of his coach companions until he dried out. He pushed his way into the Negro-only washroom and was comforted by the solitude of the closed room. He locked the door from the inside, took a seat on the lone toilet stool, and rested his elbows on his knees, his chin propped up by a balled fist.

He spent the remainder of his trip locked in the washroom and emerged only when he heard the conductor calling out his destination. And then he walked briskly into the coach and was relieved to see that the seat where the old woman had squatted was empty. He sensed that he was being watched and turned to face the accusing glare of the woman at the back of the train. She pulled her children closer to her without taking her eyes off him. He looked away, quickly gathered up his luggage, and stepped off the train into the near overpowering humidity of the summer night. His pants leg stuck uncomfortably to his leg.

Suddenly he had to piss again. Panic swept over him in a chilly wave. Why hadn't he gone before he got off the train?! He had no answer and felt betrayed by his own body. Still, he had to piss and shuffled his feet in the soft dirt beside the railroad tracks, searching the dark face of the wood-frame station for the Negro-only sign. When he discovered that there was no Negro-only facility in the small station his panic turned to anger. He lurked in the dark shadows behind the station and watched the door to the white-only bathroom for a nervous ten minutes before he found the nerve to carry out his bizarre scheme.

It was late and only the station manager lounged in the station, his feet propped on his desk, a fan buzzing noisily in his face.

He watched the station manager from the side window of the station and then swallowed back his fear and slipped into the dark interior of the room marked "White Only." The smell of stale urine and shit rushed up to meet him and he stumbled back against the closed door. He held his breath and fumbled for the doorknob, his thoughts on fresh air and flight. But the pressure at his groin sparked the anger that bubbled in his memory and he groped in the darkness for toilet paper and paper towels, which he crumpled and spread over the floor and the toilet stool. His lungs were about to burst, and he pulled his cigarette lighter from his pocket and ran his thumb over the ridged wheel. The flickering flame cast dancing shadows of the grimy walls. He applied the flame to the corners of swatches of paper and grinned broadly as the tiny tongues of fire consumed the crumpled paper to become a small blaze.

He ran from the washroom and picked up his luggage in full stride. He ran and his feet slipped over the loose dirt and gravel behind the station. When he gained the cover of the thick brush on the opposite side of the tracks, he paused and looked back to the station. Flames had chewed through the dry wood of the station wall. He heard the station manager bellow from the wide porch and then cursed himself as a warm river ran down his leg and into his shoe. *He had forgotten to piss!*

In the darkness of the brush he opened his suitcase and changed pants. Dry and fulfilled by his strike against the racist codes of the South he strolled casually by the crowd gathered around the gleaming red fire engine that had come in answer to the station manager's frantic call. He hummed "We Shall Overcome" under his breath and put in a phone call to the headquarters of the student group with whom he would spend his summer working on the voter registration drive.

He watched the dark figures fighting the fire, which had already destroyed the white-only washroom and threatened the rest of the station, and he thought of the woman on the train who had smirked at him and wondered what she would think of him then, after he had *triumphed,* even at the sacrifice of a little pride.

His entrance into the South had been marked by fire, and that fiery note became a symbol of revolution for him, or so he believed until his confinement.

That first summer in Briarville, a small but growing town in the Deep South, was one of discontent. The fever of liberation that had prompted him to come south and work for the civil rights of the darker masses cooled, and his spirit withered in the choking summer heat.

He, like the other young, idealistic freedom fighters who had come to liberate the people of the South, was quickly disillusioned, unable to cope with the stiff resistance to change that plagued both friend and foe alike. Maybe it was something in the weather or the water, which smelled of rotting eggs, that kept a stranglehold on the forces of change. But it was there in Briarville, and especially the Quarters, where he became racially and culturally alert and aware, a painful rebirth in the eye of the storm; and he quickly learned there was more to liberation, to revolution, than damning old Tarzan movies, putting one's best foot forward as a credit to the race, and screaming out, "I'm black and I'm proud." There was drudgery, disappointment, apathy, and the constant threat posed by the knights of terror. He learned to respect the fear that danced in the eyes of the people who populated the Quarters. It became his own.

A town of fifteen thousand souls, the majority of African descent, Briarville was bounded on the south and east by the muddy expanse of Pike's River, which rolled in lazy brown swells just beyond the earthen dams that protected the town from being flooded by a lazy river turned angry during the rainy season.

Almost everyone in Briarville took their lead from the river and moved slowly, almost listlessly. Their hatreds, founded in tradition ancient as the river, ran deep and wide and calm like Pike's River, until the whirlpools swirling just under the placid surface were enraged by the first hint of change.

The people of the Quarters named the river after Reverend Nehemiah Pike, who had been the spiritual leader of Golgotha Baptist Church of the Divine Savior, a ramshackle two-room shanty perched on Pike's Mountain, an oversized hill that was the only high ground in Briarville County.

Even the children of Briarville, he found, immortalized Reverend Nehemiah Pike in their play with a rather simple game, in which the leader played Reverend Nehemiah, mounting a crate pulpit, his back to his "Amen Corner" of shiny brown faces. The object of the game, he learned after long hours of watching the children play in the humid afternoons, was to reach Pike's Mountain, the crate, before the flood waters took over the low ground. The high-ground seekers were only allowed to move forward when the leader's back was to them, and he alternately spun around to face them, to catch them moving, at his own whim.

Sometimes late into the summer nights he heard the warming laughter of children at play, their voices carrying across the Quarters and muted by the thick forests that separated the Quarters from Briarville proper.

"You can come on up Pike's Mountain if you please," the leader would call out, "but you gotta come up Pike's Mountain on your knees!" The leader would pause and then shout out, "The water's rising to one foot over the dam!" And then he would spin around to spot movement among his congregation. Those caught moving, or not on their knees, were forced to return to the beginning of the game. "You gotta go back," the leader would charge those caught moving, "I seen you tryin' to walk. The water got you. You gotta go back. You gotta go back!" There would always be protests. "You know you wrong. You ain't seen me movin'." But the leader had the final say, "You go back or you out the game! That's all. You all the time tryin' to mess up something for someone else."

The confrontation would end and the game would go on with the leader repeating his spiel, "You can come on up Pike's Mountain if you please, but you gotta come up Pike's Mountain on your knees." And the leader would repeat the spiel, changing rhythm and speed of delivery in hopes of throwing his congregation off, until the water level had reached ten feet high or until he was pushed off of his pulpit by a member of the Amen Corner who timed his or her moves so as not to be caught by the eyes of the leader.

An old drunk in the Quarters told him the "true fac's" about Reverend Nehemiah, who had been confined for almost fifteen years in "Limbo," the State Asylum for the Mentally Ill.

"Reveren' Nehemiah Pike," the drunk said, his brown eyes glassy with drink, his tongue thick and eternally dry, "he wasn't crazy as a lot of folks want to believe. But that ain't to say what he did wasn't crazy…, know what I mean?" His thick tongue licked lazily from beneath his lips as he paused to gather his thoughts and push away the drink-induced film coating his memory. "No, I believes Reverend Pike had them all fooled but it didn't do him much good. Crazy or not he ended up the same place."

"Why did they confine Reverend Pike?" he had pressed, feeling that he was to become privy to a skeleton in the Briarville County closet. "What did he do that was taken as being so crazy?" He wondered too why the well-polished children of the more affluent of the darker population of Briarville, who shunned the Quarters, never played Pike's Mountain.

"Ain't so much what *he* did," the drunk said, "but what he tried to make other folks do, black folks and white folks, that started all the excitement."

"What kind of excitement?" he had asked, irritated by the drunk's slow and uneven delivery. "A riot?"

"Started out about like that," the drunk perked up as the fog lifted, clearing his memory. He leaned his chair back against the jukebox behind him, which moaned a slow blues from its lighted belly, and then motioned for the bartender to bring him another drink. "Most of the folks thought we was gonna have us a full-scale war."

"Black against white," he interjected .

"You might have expected that's the way it would go down," he drawled and then swallowed down in one gulp half of the glass of beer the bartender placed before him. "But it didn't turn out to be jus' white folks against black folks. It jus' didn't turn out to be that simple."

"Don't let this old fool lie you out of yo' money, warned the thin bartender/owner, who he learned did not live in the Quarters. "He hasn't been sober in fifteen years. "

"And long as the drinks hold out I don't ever intend to be sober," the drunk countered and finished his beer, only to stare somberly at the bottom of the glass as he sloshed around the final corner of yellow liquid, as if hoping he might somehow conjure a full glass by the effort. "Ain't no reason to be sober. A sober man's got him too much to worry about. He got to worry over what he say, might say, or done said. He got to worry over how he look and how other people think he look. He got to worry about whether he doing the right thing or going in the right direction. He got to worry about family and friends, and wives and children and taxes and jobs and rent and every damn thing else that drive a man to drink. But he can't drink. Because if he do, well, he gonna be jus' like me. And a many of them would rather be dead or crazy than like me. Me, I jus' got one problem to worry about, staying drunk."

"What about white people? Don't you worry about them?" He was irritated because the drunk was straying away from the subject of Reverend Pike. "What did *they* think about Reverend Pike? "

The bartender had long since returned to his place behind the bar. He shook his head slowly, disapprovingly from side to side and then opened the cash register and counted his money.

"I don't worry about white folks because white folks don't worry about me," the drunk explained and then smiled, flashing broken brown teeth. "They don't be worryin' over no drunks. I ain't no threat to nobody, leastways they don't think so. What they care about me when all I needs me is another drink? Don't give a damn about white women or white jobs or nothing. Know what I mean?"

He offered, "I guess so," but really didn't understand. "Was Reverend Nehemiah a threat?"

"Me and him was the same in a lot of ways," he started.

"Pike drank?!"

"Never said nothing like that." He was immediately defensive. "I ain't the one to put no badmouth on Reverend Pike when it comes to drinking. I don't know whether he did or didn't. Didn't make no real difference."

"But you said...."

"I know what I said," the drunk blustered. "I always *know* what I say. I may not be educated but I got a lot more sense than folks give me credit for, especially them niggers who be thinking they Mr. and Mrs. Hot-stuff 'cause the white folks let them move out the Quarters." The drunk cast an angry glare at the bartender, who glared back. The confrontation lasted a short moment and the drunk turned back to his line of conversation as if he had never stopped. "I got plenty of sense. That's why I know Reverend Pike wasn't really crazy, leastways not in the way they said he was. No, not Reverend Pike. He knew what he was doing and damn near scared the shit out of everybody in Briarville County doing it."

"What did he do?!" he demanded, and he turned to meet the bartender/owner's I-told-you-so smile.

"Ain't you never learned no respect for yo' elders?!" the drunk snapped back and, mouthing each word carefully, added, "Where do you come off raising you voice to me like that? You think you white or something?"

"I'm sorry," he blurted quickly, mopping perspiration from his forehead. "It's just this damn heat. I guess I just can't take it. You know."

The drunk beamed and nodded to the bartender. "Guess we both need a little something to fight this killing heat. Though it sure ain't nowhere near as hot as it was back in…."

"Two more beers," he called to the bartender, then turned back to the drunk and said "What about Pike? What did he do that caused so much trouble?"

"Like I said," the drunk began, his thick tongue snaking out over his lips in anticipation of the beer, "Reverend Nehemiah was much like me—and what I mean by that is that he didn't much care what folks thought about him—you know, the way he looked or talked or nothing like that. He just didn't care, like I don't care, you know. A man got a right to be what he want to be, if *he* can stand to smell *himself.*"

"Reverend Pike was a radical?" he encouraged.

"Wouldn't call him nothing that serious. Wasn't like he believed in no communism or no radical stuff like that. He jus' had his own way of doing things, like when the river flooded the county, damn near washing away everybody and everything in its way."

"What did Pike do?" he felt like a scratched record. *"What did Pike do?"*

The beer came, and they both drank in silence. The drunk belched, smiled, and then took a cigarette from the pack on the table between them.

"Service ain't much here," he said loud enough for the bartender to hear, "but the beer is cold. Guess that's all that really matters when it's hot like this." He sipped the beer slowly this time. "But like I was saying about Reverend Nehemiah, he was a bold man, you know. Didn't take nothing off nobody, including them white folks downtown and them dichty niggers in Little Briarville and across the river over at the college for the colored. And when the river swole up from a month of rain, Reverend Nehemiah showed everybody around here just what kind of man he was."

He formed the question with his eyes, a plea, and the drunk smiled knowingly and rambled on.

"When the river busted over the levees, folks

40

thought it was the end until they remembered Pike's Mountain, which is the only high ground in these parts." He swallowed down another mouthful of beer and puffed contentedly on the soggy end of his cigarette. "But they's only one way up Pike's Mountain, and that's a little old footpath that twists up around through the trees and then to the top of the mountain. And you know where that little old footpath begins at?"

"I'm afraid not."

There was a long pause. The glowing jukebox stood silent and there was only the sound of the large fan that rotated slowly from the ceiling. He was on edge and wasn't sure why. Someone walked slowly over to the jukebox, deposited a coin, and a sudden surge of funky blues bellowed from the speakers.

The drunk leaned forward and rested his elbows on the small table. He whispered evenly as if divulging a well-protected secret. "That footpath is down at the end of the Quartas where Little Cotton Road curves off and goes back to the main road."

He pictured Cotton Road, the main thoroughfare linking Briarville County to the state highway, and then pictured the spot where Little Cotton Road forked off from paved Cotton Road, which curved around the thick pine forest and away from the Quarters, along the earthen dams holding back the river and into Briarville proper, where whites had established the county seat. Little Cotton Road was no more than a dirt road that turned to a muddy quagmire when the weather turned bad. It serviced only the Quarters and was used by whites, and those Negroes from across the river only when Cotton Road was closed. And, he found later, the paved Cotton Road was often closed during the rainy season, even when the threat of floods was not apparent, and whites were forced to brave the ruts and muddy uncertainty of Little Cotton Road, where dark faces glared at them as they drove by.

"When the waters got to rising," the drunk continued, "the black folks and white folks got to running. And they was all running for that little footpath that ran up Pike's Mountain. Well, the Quarters niggers was the first to get there and they wasn't particular about letting white folks, or them niggers from across the river at the college, come up *their* footpath. Folks was getting their guns, and the high sheriff told the niggers that they better stand aside and let their betters go up first. I don't know what got into them niggers; maybe it was they was more afraid of the river than the white folks."

"Where were you?" he asked. "Did you get a gun? Were you ready to fight the whites for access to the road, I mean path?"

"I done my fighting long time ago—in the big war, you know. Lost the taste for fighting. And I wasn't about to stand there in all that rain when the river was rising. I climbed up that pathway on my knees, praying every inch of the way."

"I don't understand. You crawled up the mountain on your *knees?*" He recalled the words of the spiel used by the children at play. *"You can come up Pike's Mountain if you please, but you got to come up Pike's Mountain on your knees."* Were they singing about the drunk? It didn't make sense. He knew his impatience was showing. He bit down hard on his lip until he tasted blood and swallowed down a mouthful of beer that had turned flat in the heat.

"That's the way Reverend Pike wanted it." The drunk pulled back, took in the bar, and then continued, saying, "He stood up there at the top of the mountain with a double-barreled shotgun and told everybody in Briarville County that the onliest way he was going to let them come up that mountain was on their knees, praying for forgiveness for all the foolishness they was about."

"Foolishness?" he asked. "What in particular did he have in mind?"

"Reverend Pike was upset about this whole race issue, you know." He looked off thoughtfully, forming words in his mind that would express what he felt, what he remembered. "And he told them they better stop acting like a bunch of kids fussin' over who's better than who. He said they was all cut from the same bolt of cloth."

"Did they listen?" He was sorry that he couldn't have been there to bear witness to Reverend Pike's stand. He wanted more from the drunk and waved for the bartender to bring another round of beers.

"Sho'." He smiled. "Everybody listened. And after they listened they, at least the white folks, told

Reverend Nehemiah that he'd better bring his black ass on off that hill before they blew his black ass into the next county. But it didn't do much good," he confided. "Reverend Nehemiah fired off a couple of rounds from that old shotgun and the blast echoed through them trees like the thundering voice of God. And he told them that they'd better all start *treading water* or get down on their knees and crawl up that mountain with the spirit of brotherly love in their hearts and souls."

"Did they?" he asked, excited, his imagination running wild with the spectacle of Reverend Pike administering brotherly love from the muzzle of a double-barreled shotgun. "Did they do what he asked? Did they crawl up the mountain?"

"A few folks did, but most folks didn't," he said matter-of-factly. "You see, it was like this," he went on, leaning forward. "Reverend Nehemiah didn't have no big congregation, you know. Wasn't too many people ready to walk up that narrow footpath every Sunday morning in they good clothes. And the ones that did was generally not worth much. They couldn't go nowheres else."

"So what happened?" Fiery fingers tickled his spine. "Did he fight them?"

"Like I was tryin' to say," the drunk blustered, "folks didn't much care about the mountain preacher one way or the other. Fac' is, most of them already thought he was ready to be put away. But as long as he was up on that mountain, didn't nobody pay him much 'tention. So, except for me, who wasn't about to try and learn to swim, and a few others, the rest of the folks, black ones and white ones, Quarters folks and college folks, got together and tried to rush that preacher off the mountain. But the preacher let loose with both barrels of that shotgun and niggers and white folks got to rolling down that footpath like marbles. You couldn't think for all the hollering. It took 'em a little while to find out that wasn't nobody kilt. The preacher just loaded that shotgun with some nasty ol' rock salt and fired 'em up good."

He was laughing loudly; his stomach cramped; his eyes watered heavily. He didn't know whether or not the old drunk was lying to him; at the moment it really didn't matter. Reverend Nehemiah Pike was *all right* with him.

"H-how long did h-he hold off?" he managed between body-shaking fits of laughter. "R-rock salt. It's, it's unreal. Damn, I wish I had been there."

"It lasted for more than five hours," the story-teller went on. "I'm tellin' you jus' like I saw it, too. And Reverend Pike kept blasting away with that shotgun and yelling, 'come on up here, white folks,' and, 'come on up here, black folks, before you gits more than yo' feet wet. But you got to come up two-by-two, black and white, on your knees!'" The drunk talked faster. He had gotten a rise out of his one-man audience and more attention than had been given him since he could remember. "Told 'em jus' like I'm tellin' you. 'Come up the hill black and white, two-by-two, or git drowned.' And told 'em he didn't want no runnin', didn't want no tall-walkin', no pushin' and shovin'."

He tried to pick up the rhythm of a preacher but his tongue got in the way, the words bursting from his mouth in sprays of spittle. "He didn't want no unbrotherly action from nobody, and he meant *nobody*. And every time a head popped up he'd blast away with that shotgun, *kaboom, kaboom*. And them folks would scatter like a pack of scared rabbits, running through them trees, duckin' and fallin' down and cryin' for God, they mamas, and no tellin' who else."

He paused and went serious, his eyes downcast, his voice hard, cold. "But the good times didn't last. They kept on rushin' him and finally one big ol' nigger and a redneck deputy got up behind the preacher and knocked him cold with a rifle butt." He paused again, toyed with his empty beer glass. "Guess it was a lucky thing they didn't kill the preacher. They could have. And the way everybody, and I mean everybody, was screamin' for his blood so they could git away from them rising waters— hell, they could'a killed Jesus and wouldn't nobody have raised a hand or voice in his defense."

"Would you have helped?" he asked and was immediately sorry that he intruded on the drunk's private domain. "I mean...."

"I know what you mean," he said flatly. "And I done thought it over many a time. Maybe it would have been fun to be up there with the preacher, blasting away at some of these fools on both sides of the color line. But when I think about what he was trying to do and how it turned out, well, I think it's best just to let those folks who is concerned about such things deal with them. I got other problems."

"And they had him committed?"

"Trucked him off to the crazy house before the rain stopped good."

"Didn't anyone try to help him out?"

"Folks was pretty mad about the whole thing, you know." He shook his head slowly from side to side and then said in a very deliberate tone, his eyes showing intense under bushy eyebrows, "They could'a killed him, you know." He stared blankly for a moment and then smiled and blurted, *"Kaboooom! Kaboooom! Kaboooom!"* He laughed. *"Kabooom! Kaboooom! Kaboooom!* And they ran like hell."

"Elmo! You cut that damn drunken bellowing or get out of my place!" came from the direction of the bar.

The drunken Elmo ignored the command; his eyes and voice softened and he said, "God, it was great. Ain't nothin' like that happened around here in a long time."

Elmo fell silent, momentarily comforted by his memories.

The Blue Bird Bar and Grill wasn't a fashionable place. In fact, except for the jukebox and the ceiling fan, the bar had little to offer by way of atmosphere. He stared at Elmo and then excused himself from the table, saying, "Got to take a leak."

The toilet was out back. He walked drunkenly towards the back door to the bar, the sound of the blues in his ears. He gained the back door when he heard two men arguing at the table near the bar.

"I'm tellin' you, all that nonviolent shit ain't gonna work on no rednecks. They eat that shit up. They scared to death of a nigger that show some balls."

"Maybe so, maybe not. But it don't make no sense for us to be tryin' to start no mess wit' the white folks. Things ain't been so bad here in Briarville County. But I kind of got to give them youngsters credit for coming down here and tryin' to do something to change things."

"Nonviolent folks! When has a cracker ever been nonviolent? Huh? You jus' answer me that."

"I ain't got no argument agin that."

"You got that right! But as long as they keep their pasty faces out of my way, ain't gonna be no problems. Got something for the first one steps out of line with me. Cracker put his white-ass hands on me and he'll beat me to the Devil's door."

"But you won't be but a half a step behin', nigger. You all fat and no meat. You know you ain't 'bout to mess with them white folks. You think you so bad, take your bad black ass on downtown and talk that stuff to them white folks."

"Man, what you talkin'? I ain't lost a damn thing downtown. I figures them crackers got as much right to hate me as I got to hate them. That's the natural way of it. Fair exchange ain't never been no robbery. I'm tellin' you what I know."

"Nigger, you ain't no different than any other body. You scared, too. Scared this thing these kids is tryin' to do to make things right is gonna git out of hand and you gonna be forced to face them white folks whether you want to or not."

"I do what I want to do!"

"You do just what white folks force on you, like the rest of us. You tell all that other stuff to some-body who ain't crawled along the same road wit' you."

"Awww, leave me the hell alone. You talkin' crazy!"

He felt better after his trip to the outhouse behind the bar. Elmo greeted him with a drunken nod and slipped back into his silent reverie. He bought a bot-tle of whiskey and Elmo's eyes perked up. They drank late into the night, holding an impromptu trib-ute to the memory of Reverend Nehemiah Pike, one-time king of Pike's Mountain. They drank and laughed too loudly, and drew angry looks from the bartender and the crowd of customers who crowd-ed the smoky interior of the club.

It was Saturday night for them all, he thought. They drank more whiskey and listened to the funky lowdown blues that oozed from the jukebox and folded over them like hot syrup.

"What's up there?" he asked. "On the mountain? Is Reverend Pike's church still there?"

"Nope," Elmo belched, "fools burned the damn thing to the ground. I didn't think they could git no fire going real good in all that rain, but some nigger found the gasoline the Reverend used for his generator and they poured gas on his hymn books and everything else until they got the fire going real good. It didn't take long before that little ol' church was just a pile of wet black ashes. And *they* said the preacher was crazy. They burned down the only shelter that was up there and, man, the rain was coming down in buckets."

"But what's up there, now?"

"Don't know! Don't know nobody that goes up there. Ain't really no reason to go up there now that the preacher and the church ain't there no more. Thought to go up there myself a couple of times, you know, take a look around. But they's jus' that little footpath, and it's all tangled over with brush. Maybe jus' that pile of black ashes, don't know for sure. The only use anybody got for that place is to git away from the river when it rises. But they got the dams built better now. Jus' ain't no need for that high ground."

It may have been the mixture of beer and whiskey, or just that he needed a break from the monotony of the parade of long, hot summer nights; though he preferred to believe that his actions that night were triggered more by a deeply felt obligation to do something—something *spectacular*—in the memory of Reverend Pike, *American hero*. Whatever the case, he spent the last of his money on another bottle of whiskey and, failing to induce Elmo to join him on a climb to the top of Pike's Mountain, cradled the bottle in his arms and stumbled out of the club and onto Little Cotton Road, the rutted ribbon of dirt that wound through the tangle of weather-beaten shacks that made up the Quarters.

It was late but people milled about, laughed, drank, or sat solemnly on their darkened porches watching the "sinners" go through their Saturday night routines. The Quarters on Saturday nights was the most democratic place in the whole county. In the Quarters no one was better than anyone else.

The footpath that wound to the top of Pike's Mountain began where Little Cotton Road curved away from the Quarters and passed by a series of stately relics of pre-Civil-War architecture where some of the prominent members of the faculty of the colored college across the river made their homes. There the dirt road became a gravel street, bordered by wooden walkways and neat white picket fences. At the place where the railroad tracks crossed the gravel road, a large, professionally rendered sign stood sentinel and announced in bold red lettering over a Briarville County municipal code number:

NIGGER!
DON'T LET THE SUN SET ON YOU
ON THE WRONG SIDE OF THE TRACKS!

He found that it was an ambiguous imperative, obeyed or ignored solely depending on the economic, political, and sexual circumstances that alternatively linked and polarized the divergent communities.

The footpath was partially covered over with thick growth. He swallowed a mouthful of whiskey and started up, stumbling, falling, tumbling off the path and crashing into the thorny brush. More than once he thought to turn back and, panting heavily, bleeding from the countless bruises and scratches and cuts that covered his body, he stood in the soft glow of the moonlight that filtered through the trees like beacons from heaven and squinted against the darkness ahead, plotting a course up the narrow trail that disappeared into thick brush every few feet. Though it was little more than a tree-and-brush-covered hill, the climb was steep. But the whiskey numbed him against the pain that wracked his body, and the picture of Reverend Nehemiah Pike blasting away with his shotgun in the name of peace and brotherhood renewed his interest in reaching the top of the mountain.

Time ticked by slowly, monitored by night sounds that blended somehow with the laughter and the music floating up from the Quarters below. He had no way of telling how long it took him to reach the top, or what time it was when he got there. The stars shone brightly above the tops of the trees and the moon painted a soft yellow pool in the center of the clearing that was little bigger than a football field. A rustling in the brush beside him made him think of snakes, and he stepped quickly and uncertainly away from the suspect brush, his feet barely scraping the ground as he broke into a rubbery-legged run.

His heart pounded, his throat was dry, his clothes stuck uncomfortably to his body. He drank from the bottle he had held in a death grip throughout the climb and fumbled for a cigarette. When the pounding in his chest eased he breathed more easily and furtively glanced around. He didn't know what he expected to find, maybe the black pile of ashes that would mark the sight of Golgotha Baptist Church of the Divine Savior.

Off to one side of the clearing he saw what appeared to be a wall crumbling in disrepair. He wondered if the preacher had dug the well himself and had started towards its dark shape when he noticed three large objects at the far end of the clearing where the trees let moonlight filter through like the beams from dozens of flashlights. From his vantage point they looked like enclosed telephone booths. But as he came closer to them he recognized them for what they were, *chemical outhouses!*

Had Reverend Nehemiah Pike built them? he asked himself and then turned angry as he made out the Briarville County seal above lettering that read: "WHITE ONLY".

He read the lettering on each of the outhouses, it was the same: "WHITE ONLY". What were the niggers supposed to do? he thought. *Squat behind trees?*

He knew what he had to do, *had to do!* And he knew then that it would be the most spectacular and symbolic act he could perform in tribute to the king of Pike's Mountain. Tingling with excitement and buoyed by the whiskey, he scrambled around collecting dried brush and wood and piled it inside and all around the three chemical toilets. He laughed, giggled, drank whiskey, and then rested on a nearby stump, bathed in moonlight after having prepared his bonfire tribute.

He sat on the stump and rocked back and forth, singing, at first under his breath, then more loudly, more broadly, "God gave Moses the rainbow sign, no more water, the fire next time!" And he laughed and danced around the stump shouting, "Kabooooom! Kaboooooom! Kaboooooom!" to the trees, to the sky, to the three outhouses that sat solemnly in the glow with "WHITE ONLY" on their faces. *"Kaboooooom! Kaboooooom! Kabooooooomboooomboooom!"* he shouted and danced until he fell into a sweaty heap.

He lay on the cool ground for what seemed an hour and then, seeing the first hint of the approaching day, deliberately set about lighting his tribute to Reverend Pike.

The outhouses burned brightly. He sat on the stump and watched in silence until the fires reached their hottest point. Would anyone come? he wondered. And if caught how would he explain his presence there? But no one came. The fires died down as the morning sun peaked over the trees, and by the time he felt the first warm rays of sunlight, the three outhouses were only a pile of smoldering black ashes. And when the sun started its climb up the sky, he stood and raised his voice to sing in a cracked and off-key falsetto: *"Lift every voice and sing 'til earth and heaven ring, ring with the harmony of liberty...."*

And as he sang out he heard church bells chiming from down below in Little Briarville and Briarville proper. And he sang the more loudly: *"Let our rejoicing rise, high as the listening skies. Let it resound loud as the rolling sea!"*

And then he ended his tribute to Reverend Pike with a rasping delivery of "We Shall Overcome."

At the time, he did not entertain the thought that he would ever meet Reverend Nehemiah Pike, but fate had planned otherwise and he would find that the coarse voice that trumpeted his entrance into Limbo was the voice of the Reverend Nehemiah Pike.

The darkness crashed by outside the window of the train as it hurtled westward through the night. The veil slipped back in place and he was alone again, in the present, and uncertainty dug a deep pit in his stomach. At least in the past, though painful, there was a predictability that was soothing. He wanted to disappear into the padding of the chair, take up as little space as possible until he found a place where he could stretch out, just a little. Maybe everyone was right. Maybe things had changed and he was harboring a bitter urge for revenge against those who had confined him and tagged him insane. Maybe the war was finally over and he, a returning POW, would have to learn to shelve his bitter feelings and find a way of fitting into the "brave new world" of free and equal people.

He was going home, and he was free. The release papers in his hand documented that fact. That was all that counted. And though he felt that heavy shackles had been cut from his arms and legs, he could only stare into the darkness, afraid to make contact with the outside world.

He slipped into a fitful sleep and dreamed of a valley below the purple mountains, and trains, and old Nehemiah. In the valley below the purple mountains, pot-bellied steam engines trailed white plumes of steam; chugging coal-burners belched clouds of black smoke; diesels growled and bellowed; sleek, silver streamliners hummed before the pack leading the way towards a tiny white beacon of light in the face of a purple mountain. Jutting up from a corner of the valley, yet dwarfed by the purple mountains, was a glass skyscraper. A huge television antenna protruded from the roof of the skyscraper, and perched on the spiny arms of the antenna like a grounded vulture was a nude fat woman. A clone of Aunt Jemima and Lady Liberty, she wore a crown of dry twigs over a red scarf and banged a tambourine against her flabby thighs. She cried out in a monotonous sing-song, *"Git on board, little children. Git on board, little children. Git on board, little children. There's room for many a more!"*

Like long lines of ragged refugees, hordes of faceless people, their lives carried in greasy shopping bags, answered the call and trooped from subterranean passages, pushing, clawing, cursing, and punching to be first in line, or at least a space closer to the head of the line.

From her perch the fat nude clanged her tambourine and swayed on her roost, singing out the more loudly in her flat voice, *"Git on board, little children. Git on board, little children. Git on board, little children. There's room for many a more!"*

Train whistles screeched and screamed from the bowels of the valley to clash against the wailing and crying and cursing of the ragtag mob now running after the moving trains, urged on by sequined rock trios fronting as blues singers who were in the know crooning, *"Git on board, little children. Git on board, little children."* And men in brightly colored silk suits held foreign language bibles close to their chests and intoned, *"There's room for many a more! There's room for many a more!"*

Ripping at each other's clothes, the refugee men, women, and children tumbled over fallen bodies, and their torn pieces of clothing fluttered like drunken butterflies above them. Dark clouds hovered over the valley, and above the dark clouds a mechanical hand wiggled steely fingers in synch to the sing-song chant, and the naked fat woman, her tambourine setting the monotonous rhythm, danced spastically like a puppet on a string.

A disembodied voice crackled above the dark clouds, and the purple mountains shuddered like great mounds of grape jello. *"Run, niggers, run!"* the mechanical voice commanded. And the naked Jemima/Liberty cried out, *"There's room for many a more! There's room for many a more!"*

And the refugees ran and joined the chanting nude in her ditty, *"There's room for many a more! There's room for many a more!"* And the voice from above cracked, *"Run, niggers, run!"* And they ran like frightened chickens, stretching for the trains racing over the gleaming tracks.

Suddenly a bright light broke through the clouds and centered in the light was the face of Reverend Nehemiah Pike, cracked and weathered like the skin of an old leather jacket, the eyes sparkling like black pearls, and he spoke and the purple mountains parted and a raging river flooded the valley and the trains, and the hordes of refugees disappeared under the dark waters, leaving only the face of Reverend Nehemiah Pike, his hair like a tuft of pure white cotton, his eyes now intense, piercing.

"You a marked nigger!" Reverend Nehemiah charged. "A crazy nigger! Dangerous to yourself and *everydambodyelse.* You out yo' cage now. And you ready to run again. So, run, nigger! Run! That's why they turned you loose, so you can run some more. If you believe they lies, run! It's a white man's world! You believe that? Black folks was born to run before the white man's gun! You believe that?! You ain't white! You can *believe* that! That's at least one natural fac'. But if you git the right angle on things and understand what you here for, what's expected of you, you'll have a lot less to worry over when you do what you gonna have to do."

He heard himself ask, "What?"

"Live, boy! You got some notion you ain't got to keep on trying to live 'til you die?! Boy, you ain't got many options 'til you see who you are. And dying is the least pleasant of the two. So live, scrawny little rabbit who ain't learned how to duck a chunked rock. Live! You a *badniggercrazyrabbit* and even the other running rabbits don't want to run with you. You got to be smart if you want to live. They done give you yo' life. Live it the best you can. Can't nobody demand more of a man than that. Hell, if you can't tear the prison down, don't mean you have to let it tear you down! Do the time, boy! If you gonna live to be a man. Red folks, brown folks, yellow folks, black folks, and even white folks—they all got time to do. Ain't nobody different in that respect. You got to find a way to do your time 'til you can break out the box like a natural man. Don't no smart rabbit go runnin' lickety-split through no strange briar patch 'til he know the way! A smart rabbit cares that the fish don't bite if the fisherman got a gun! You got a breathing space to worry about. Carry it with you, that's the natural way, and you'll find your own space. Don't you know, dead men's bones is rattled by the living!?"

He woke in a cold sweat. The first rays of daylight slithered through the window of the train like a golden snake.

And suddenly he recognized how much he missed Reverend Nehemiah Pike, who had made his stand on his mountain and then provided spiritual direction for the inmates of Limbo until he died. In a weed-choked plot of red dirt behind the asylum, a small white cross marked Reverend Nehemiah Pike's space.

They said Reverend Pike was crazy because of his obsession with the river. Maybe he was crazy, but it didn't matter; he made more sense than many of the people he had met.

"The river was here first," Pike had told him. "It was here first and it's got a mind of its own. Made up long before any of us was ever thought of. Respect that mind and you got a chance of making it. But if you get too cocky and want to run against the flow of the river, you'll get dragged under before you git to…."

"Where?" he had asked.

"To the end, or the beginning, depending on which way you trying to go."

"Of the river?!"

"Naw, fool!" Nehemiah had countered. "The

river's got no end. It goes on and on until somebody dams it or dries it up."

"To the end of what then?!"

"The time you got to do!"

"How much time?"

"I don't *know* how much time!" Nehemiah didn't
like questions. He said what he had to say and questions would not coax any more from him, unless he
had planned to say it anyway. "That's written in a
book I ain't never seen. Don't think I want to see
it either. Might take some of the bite out of life. Be
like a rowboat ride in a swimming hole."

And in moments of deep inspiration he said, "The
river is everything. It's life and death and all that
counts in between. Some folks say we crawled out
the oceans and the rivers. Maybe so. Maybe not. I
spec' that we was born in them to stay. The one
thing I know is you got to learn to ride the river,
not tame it. A tame river ain't nothing but a trench
filled with stagnant water. You got to keep some
action going. Learn to ride the river or make waves
in a tame one, and maybe you'll make it."

The lush green tangle of the South was behind
him. The landscape had changed drastically to dusty
rolling hills and flat expanses of farmlands and
grazing lands. He was going home, that's all that
counted.

He was finally going home.

And maybe if he had not decided to stay in the
South—and it would be a thought that would haunt
him continually—maybe if he hadn't stayed in the

South and decided to enroll in the colored college across the river, his life might have been quite different. But then he never would have met and learned from Reverend Nehemiah Pike.

TWO

MAMA'S MILK

The sharp cry of a siren invaded the icy bedroom. He jerked awake and blinked against the pale gray rays of morning light filtering through the sheer tan curtains shielding the windows. He heard a baby's crying, and the mechanical wail of the siren took precedence over the baby's crying until the piercing screech faded into the distance.

He lay motionless, his eyes open but unfocused. Home or asylum? Swallowing down the lump clogging his throat, he counted slowly from *one* and then pushed himself up from the bed and focused in on his space when he reached the count of eight. *Home!*

The walls were pale green, plaster and concrete block, sturdy as any prison. He trembled in the morning chill and slowly, methodically, took in each corner of the room. The dresser was familiar, even the bed, the drab wall, yet everything seemed strange and he longed for the familiar world of the asylum and the security of long-established routine.

The longing passed when he saw the crumpled release papers on the night stand near his bed and he sat in the middle of the bed and rocked slowly backwards and forwards and whispered in a cracked voice, "I'm home! I'm home! I'm home!" Back where it all began. Where he had been born and raised. Home, near his mother. Didn't that, more than anything else, make it home?

Yet he was nervous, frightened. Maybe he shouldn't have come home just as he shouldn't have stayed in the South where his troubles began. If in fact he was diseased, mentally ill, as *they* had diagnosed, instead of a political POW, as he wanted to believe, wouldn't it be dangerous for him to return to the place where he had contracted the mental disease?"

A baby cried from beyond the green walls and music erupted from somewhere in the gray gloom outside the window. He could see the upper floor of one of the apartments in the dull tan building across the way. Torn curtains sagged in the broken window. A dark face poked out from behind the curtains and bobbed for a moment like a puppet in a Punch and Judy show and then ducked back behind the curtains.

Was it a face he should know? He was *home.*

People he grew up with, went to school and drank with, learned the secrets of sex with, all lived in the drab buildings that surrounded him. But the face wasn't familiar and at that moment he couldn't recall who lived, or maybe once-lived, in the apartment across the way.

The baby cried and he heard a gruff angry voice bark, "Bitch, shut that baby up!"

"I ain't yo' bitch no more! So git yo' black ass out my bed and leave my baby alone!" The woman's voice was shrill, angry.

"You got that right, *bitch!* That baby sure ain't none of mine!"

"Ain't nothin' here belong to you, nigger! Git out my house! And quit pulling on me. You ain't gittin' no mo' pussy here!"

"Bitch, what you talkin' about?! You better turn over and act like you got some sense!"

"Leave me the hell alone!" she screamed. "Take yo' black-ass hands off of me! You ain't gittin' no mo' *pussy here!*"

"Who you fuckin'?!!"

"I ain't fuckin' nobody. And I ain't gonna fuck you!"

"Who you fuckin', bitch?! You got to be fuckin' around wit' somebody!"

"I got saved! And I ain't gonna *fornicate* no more wit'out being married! I've taken Jesus Christ as my Lord and Master."

"You fuckin' Jesus Christ?!"

"Don't be usin' Jesus' name like no curse word!"

"Bitch, *who you fuckin'?!*"

"I told you, I've been *saved!*"

"Saved from *what?!* You done lost yo' damn mind! You still sittin' up here fat and ugly wit' four babies wit' three different daddies, and you talkin' about you been *saved!* Bitch, you crazy as them Sherm Heads who be talkin' all that shit about God and religion and the Bible like they was born in a church. But it be that dust talkin' shit. You been smokin' Sherms?!"

"You know I don't do no crazy shit like that! I told you what I had to tell you. *I been saved.* And you better quit cursing Jesus."

"I'm gonna tell you what you better do, bitch. You give your *soul* to Jesus if you want to, but the *pussy* belongs to me!"

He could hear them struggling, cursing each other, and then there was silence. He pushed himself up from his bed and his stomach flip-flopped nervously. His hands were clammy. He stared at the drab green wall and wondered who won out, *Jesus or the nigger?* He rushed into his clothes, a blue denim shirt and faded jeans, and laced on a pair of high-top tennis shoes. He heard only the sound of the baby crying on the other side of the wall and music that now seemed to spring from *everywhere.*

From somewhere outside came angry voices, and he walked over to the window and looked out and down into the debris-covered parking lot between the two buildings. He saw five figures hunched over, shooting dice between a ten-year-old brown

Cadillac and a derelict Ford propped up by milk crates. They were all dressed alike, wearing baggy gray pants, white T-shirts, dark jackets, and Pittsburgh Pirates baseball caps, black with gold stripes ringing the crown. The doors of the Cadillac hung open and a funky disco blared from the radio.

"How much money you got, nigger!?"

"I got enough to cover whatever you put down, *home!*"

"I didn't ask you that. I asked you how much money you got in your pocket."

"Hey, *home,* I told you what I wanted you to know."

Two of the figures stood and faced off.

"I got yo' *homeboy* right here between my legs, nigger!" the taller of the two spat. "Now, what'd I ask you?"

The others backed away; one sat in the car, the other two leaned against the hood and watched in silence.

"Home, you messin' up the game."

The taller man moved quickly, pushing the smaller man down with his left hand and pulling a large black handgun from his waistband with his right. He straddled the downed man and pointed the barrel of the gun at his forehead. "What'd I ask you, nigger? Or do you want to smart-mouth some more!"

"I got twenty dollars!"

"Give it up before I blow yo' nappy head off!"

The downed man fumbled for the money and

gave it up with a palsied hand. The others watched silently and moved their bodies to the chaotic beat of the music blasting from the radio.

"Let me up, man!"

"I ain't decided that I ain't gonna blow yo' head off."

From above he yelled down in a scratchy voice, "Cut that out!" and was immediately sorry. The gunman swirled, stood, and pointed the gun at the bedroom window.

"Nigger, what you got to say about this?! Huh?!"

The others stared up at him; even the downed man stood and glared curiously, even angrily up at him. And he mumbled a squeaky, "N-nothing," and backed away from the window, his legs trembling, his breathing coming in jerky gasps. "Aw, shit!" he said finally and then heard a woman's voice, old, demanding: "You boys git on away from here wit' all that commotion. You don't live 'round here no way. Git on 'way from here; I done already called *the pohleece!*"

"Go fuck yo'self, old bitch!"

He heard the car doors slam and the engine roar to life. Heartbeats later the blasting music was gone and his thumping heart kicked up a pounding rhythm, and his head ached, pulsated, twisting in weird contortions like the sufferers he had seen in television commercials hawking pain killers.

He was afraid. Maybe he never should have come back. He was home and he was afraid. And he didn't understand. He stood in the morning gloom trailing through the window and lighted a cigarette from the pack on the night stand before he found the courage or enough curiosity to inch back to the window and furtively glance down into the parking lot. The brown Cadillac was gone but the haunting faces of the teenagers still lingered like a bitter memory. He felt relieved and stood just to the side of the window so that he could look out without being seen.

There was activity in the parking lot. A woman, still in her nightgown, pink and yellow rollers sprouting from her streaked red hair like the springs from a torn mattress, leaned into the driver's side of a long four-door Buick. Her hips swayed and gyrated loosely to the beat of music coming from the car's radio. He could not see the driver clearly or hear what they were saying. A small child appeared in the doorway of the apartment just behind the woman and stumbled crying out of the apartment in only her panties, and the woman jerked around and hollered, "Get your ass back in that house and stop that damn crying. Ain't nothin' the matter with you. Git back in there like I'm telling you!"

The child scrambled back into the hollow of the apartment, and the woman with the pink and yellow rollers sprouting from her head turned back to the car, her hips keeping time to the music.

An old woman looked disapprovingly from the doorway of the adjacent apartment, her large body draped in a faded red-and-yellow tent-like dress, her hair tufts of gray-black wire. She carried a large pot in her hand and wobbled off the porch to prune leaves from the towering collard-green shrubs growing in her small garden. Old Mrs. Tucker, he thought, and a tiny smile played across his trembling lips. Fannie Mae Tucker, probably the oldest woman in the projects, a stalwart presence and an immovable object. He and the other wild urchins had found a strange pleasure in raiding her well-kept garden. Her pot full, Fannie Mae Tucker ambled back onto her porch, cast an angry glare in the direction of her neighbor's rotating hips, and then went into her apartment and slammed the door behind her with a resounding bang.

From the hallway he heard his mother's voice singing a syrupy blues.

Memories rushed back, and he felt cheated, denied the warm homecoming that was his due. Things had changed, they said, and they had lied. He knew it then as he recalled the steely glares from the teenagers who had threatened him. And he remembered that the Gardens, though his home, was not the paradise he had ached to return to, escape from Limbo to, and rest until his wounds healed, until he got his program together.

Some said the blues was the National Anthem of "the Gardens," the maze of concrete-block, two-story apartment buildings that sprawled like pale green and tan barracks over acres of prime land in Los Angeles city. The blues, they said, expressed the mood, the pains, even the sporadic hopes of people in transition. Others, the angry and restless who were looking for a marching cadence, a war song, damned the blues for perpetuating and symbolizing the madness and failures of a broken people. The music belching from the faces of the apartment was frenzied, up-tempo, unlike the blues with its moaning and groaning, its biting satire.

There was a time, he was almost certain, when communication in the Gardens was rapid, musical, personal, almost unerring. They had all enjoyed a sophisticated body language, personalized by stylish hand movements, trademark grunts, quips, nods; mellow notes hummed, strummed, and drummed; quick-steps in time to a mutually heard rhythm. Originally masked as buffoonery and the gibberish of the undereducated, the mentally depraved, the economically deprived, the socially disadvantaged, by outsiders dark and light who never quite got the rhythm and the system down, "ghettoese" was shunned, until "de-souled," packaged, and commercialized into oblivion as the lyric lines for alien Wall Street musicians. Ghettoese redefined became no language at all.

But he remembered, though unwillingly, that a smalltown reclusiveness had always gripped the Gardens, where thousands flocked from small southern communities, northern ghettos, and poverty, from defeatist tags acquired as their birthright, becoming too often their reasons for being; and the reclusiveness was further complicated over abbreviated generations by an intricate network of kinship ties linking transplanted mothers, matriarchs in the past, to sons and daughters, and grandsons and granddaughters, extended families of cousins, uncles, aunts, and in-laws, legal and otherwise, and lovers and ex-lovers, which too often exploded into bloody inter-clan warfare when communication wasn't right.

And he knew that though the Gardens was envisioned as halfway houses for the poor who needed temporary asylum from hard times, somewhere along the line administrators, politicians, police officials, liberals, bleeding-heart and otherwise, conservatives, civil rights groups, and tenants alike lost sight of the intended purpose, and the Gardens became a "holding tank" for the chronically deprived until that day when some great plan would be devised to cure them of their debilitating, *self-inflicted poverty,* if not permanently secure them out of view of Americans successfully pursuing their *constitutionally guaranteed dreams.*

Over the years he watched people move in and out of the Gardens. Some sought the reclusive shield as a protection against the outside world that refused them entry. Living contradictions, they sought permanent asylum away from their dreams. And hidden behind double-deadbolt-locked doors and minds, they cursed their birth, angry, not always because of what they were told they must give up— music, culture, history, color if possible, would be willingly discarded or exchanged for passage into the outside—but more often because they were denied the opportunity to "cross over" the invisible river. Solemnly, even self-righteously, they peered from their windows, paced the tangle of littered walks and ruts worn in unkempt lawns, and indicted fellow inmates for their mutual confinement.

Some found a way to make their homes there. They lived there, gave birth and raised their children there—and hoped their children escaped.

Some had every intention of escaping themselves, when times got better. But times never got better, or life in the Gardens bad enough to make them run. They waited, occasionally growled in disgust and frustration, and dreamed their dreams in silent defiance of the dream denied them, surviving in the shadow of the "Horn of Plenty."

For too few the Gardens became a way station on the way to better things. They worked, saved, protected their children from the crippling jungle that was the Gardens, and carefully plotted their escape route from *day one*.

And from the pages of the local black press, provided over the years by his mother, he kept abreast of the still embryonic black middle class who, along with some bitter escapees scarred by the tangle of jagged and thorny edges in the Gardens, saw the Gardens, projects in general, as a symbol of a shameful past, an anchor rooting them in distorted racial perceptions—their own and others—to a kinship they would prefer to deny, and further symptomatic of their failure to secure themselves a rightful place in the American Dream machine.

As he looked out over the flat, dull buildings, he could not help but think of Limbo, with its sickly green walls and bars, and the Quarters scattered like cast-off packing crates below Pike's Mountain and out of sight of Briarville proper and the residents of Little Briarville, who preferred to take the long way around over paved Cotton Road and through Briarville city to reach their homes on the graveled section of Little Cotton Road, until those times when racial tensions and an unavoidable "skinship" forced them to use the rutted and dusty stretch of Little Cotton Road that wriggled like a dry brook through the Quarters.

The smell of frying bacon slipped under the closed door of his bedroom and he was momentarily nauseous; cigarette smoke curling upwards from the tip of the cigarette dangling from his lips watered his eyes. Blinking against the smoke, he backed away from the window and crushed his cigarette out in a small glass ashtray that bore the name of a popular Las Vegas casino.

Hesitantly he opened the bedroom door and walked out into the narrow hallway and to the bathroom. It was icy cold in the small porcelain cell, yet he perspired freely. He bent over the sink, splashed his face with cold water, and then stared at his face in the mirror above the sink.

He had spent almost a third of his life in Limbo, and his eyes were glazed pieces of brown glass in hollow sockets. His hair bore a handful of tiny silver specks that were like bits of metal shavings on a tuft of black cotton. Full lips protruded from under a broad nose, and his skin, though drawn and pale, still maintained its rich cocoa flavor.

His body was lean, even angular. In the Quarters the women had called him "poor" and in need of a cooking woman to fatten him up. He had smiled and pressed on, hearing the sound of a marrying preacher murmuring in the back of his mind.

He brushed his teeth, filled his mouth with water from the spigot, and gargled. He felt better though his head still ached. He turned the faucet to off and an irritating *plunk, plunk, plunk* echoed in the hollow of the sparkling white porcelain. He spit out the water and pounded at the faucet handle with the palm of his hand. The drip persisted its steady *plunk, plunk, plunk* and seemed to grow worse each time he hammered it with his hand.

"Is that you fumbling around up there?" he heard his mother's voice from below. "What are you doing? Are you all right?"

He sensed an urgency in her voice and barked a loud, "I'm fine," towards the closed bathroom door.

"What are you doing up there?" she called again. "Are you sure you're okay?"

"I'm fine," he shouted, irritated by her concern. He was cured! A grown man. He could take care of himself. And then he was pestered by the question, "Why did he come home?" And he couldn't answer, not right then. Maybe he came back for the same reason the other refugees huddled in the sanctuary of the Gardens. He had no place else to go to be free. "I'm just fine!" he repeated and glared at his reflected image, still shaken by the confrontation with the teenage gamblers and the possibility that he might have been senselessly shot.

The narrow stairs creaked under his weight. He heard light, hurried footsteps padding over the tile floor below and his mother met him at the bottom of the staircase, asking, "How do you feel? Are you sure you're okay?" A soft plea glimmered in her deep brown eyes. She smiled, a hesitant twitch of her full lips.

"I'm fine," he smiled. "Never felt better."

"That's good," she said. "Breakfast is almost ready. Did you wash up?"

"Yes," he said, then glanced back up the stairs. "Faucet in the bathroom is leaking."

"It's been like that for two weeks," she said. "After breakfast I'll go down to the office and put in another request for service. But there's no telling when they'll get around to fixing it."

"Maybe I can fix it," he offered, anxious to feel useful again. "Shouldn't be too hard."

"They've got a plumber that gets paid well for fixing these leaks and stoppages. Let him do it." She turned and started back to the kitchen, saying, "One of these days every sink and toilet in the projects is going to back up and drown us all."

When she spoke he heard a muted sax. Soft yet full. Strong yet mellow—like a Charles White charcoal come to life to the beat of Charlie Parker. Her nose, like his, was full and prominent yet not so broad as to take away from the delicate quality of her round face. Her skin showed few wrinkles and was a sweet mixture of soft browns, blacks, and reds—a sassy brown, even though the years seemed to have drawn circles under her brown eyes. Her hair was neatly combed back on her head, and silver streaks belied the girlish quality that still glowed in her eyes.

Suddenly he turned and bounded back up the stairs to his bedroom. He crossed to the night stand, folded the papers that released him from the custody of Limbo into a neat square, and stuffed them into the back pocket of his jeans. Taking his pack of cigarettes, he went downstairs to breakfast, though he had no taste for food.

He had gotten in late from the train station the night before and had little time to talk to his mother. He lied and said that he was tired from the long trip, but he preferred some time, a period of adjustment, before he faced anyone who might ask him to probe under the still fresh and tender scab that had formed over his past ten years. He had simply told his mother that he had suffered a nervous breakdown. He felt that it would be easier for her to accept, and he also wanted to protect her from the knowledge of what he had done. He wasn't sure that she, or any of his family, would really understand what motivated his actions, which were too readily written off as the by-products of a crazed mind. Both diagnoses pointed to the same conclusion: he was unfit to walk and work and live among so-called "normal" Americans. And the bitter rage that had sustained him over his years of confinement swelled up inside him like a great gaseous balloon, and he felt that his chest might burst open and spill his guts out onto the meticulously polished floors.

"Sit down and eat," his mother said as he walked into the kitchen. "Food's hot, and you don't look like they fed you too well in…." She hesitated, drank from a glass of what appeared to be water, then said, "that place."

"Food wasn't too bad," he said, "just didn't get enough of it sometimes. On Sundays, though, when some of the patients got visitors, we all ate very high on the hog. Southern folks believe in bringing food whenever they go visiting. I guess it's part of the culture. And your monthly care packages helped!"

"Let's not talk about that place. Just be thankful that you're back home and safe." She placed a plate of pork chops, bacon, eggs, and grits before him. "Did they treat you all right? I mean those stories we always hear about sticking electric wires in your head and doping you up—they're not really true are they? I mean people just don't do that kind of thing in America anymore. How could they?"

He knew what she wanted to hear, needed more than anything else to hear, and he lied, "Just horror stories to sell books and movies. Most of the time we spent sitting in the day room, playing dominoes, checkers, reading, looking at soap operas on the tube, or just talking, you know. Some of the people, the patients, are more interesting to talk and listen to than most of the people on the outside who are supposed to be sane. It wasn't so bad. It was like being in a peaceful rest home in the laid-back South without a worry in the world. And every now and then we'd have to talk to the doctors, look at a few ink blots—you know a couple of them looked like Uncle Snooks and Uncle Lee. How are they doing?"

"Just fine. They want to see you." She took a seat at the table and drank from her glass. "They really didn't treat you badly? They didn't try to hurt you or anything?"

"I'm as healthy and sane as I'm ever going to be." He smiled, leaned across the table, and kissed her on the cheek. "Doctors said I was fine. I feel fine. And everything in the world seems fine to me."

"Eat your breakfast," she commented with a broad smile, relieved by his lies.

"What did you tell the family?" He bit into a pork chop and the meat was a wad of cardboard in his mouth. "Did they ask what I was doing? Where I was?"

"I just told them that you were working down south and going to school," she said sheepishly. "I didn't see any reason to tell them anything else."

"Don't you think they would've understood? It happens to a lot of people. It's not contagious. People are cured every day. Sometimes it's just a matter of a little time and a little rest away from the turmoil that started the whole thing."

He felt hurt that his mother had not told the truth about his confinement. He felt forced into complicity in an elaborate lie that he did not have the strength or will to maintain. "It didn't matter to me what they thought. It was none of their business. And there really wasn't anything they could have done about it anyway."

"I guess you're right," he said weakly, knowing that he would be faced with finding a way of telling them so that he could get on about living his life.

His mother got up from the table, took a nearly empty bottle of off-brand vodka from the refrigerator, and drained the contents into a glass. She didn't look at him again until she dropped the empty bottle into the trash can in the corner and sipped from the glass of vodka.

"Kind of early, isn't it?" he asked and was immediately sorry that he had barged into her world on his first day home as if he was somehow a man with a mission. When he left he knew his mother drank too heavily, most of the time beer, though sometimes anything, especially vodka. When she drank, her voice turned syrupy, thick, and sweet, and she sang her favorite blues songs, in tribute to Dinah, Billie, and Bessie, and the countless women who had touched the same fire and lived to tell the story. And when she sang, her voice probed the shadowy corners of the blues for a shaft of light, and sketched pictures for him of a world that was as much a part of his story as hers.

She didn't die. But maybe he should have listened more closely, brushed away the sweet syrup, and faced the bitter lyrics. When she drank too much, the singing stopped, and he grew to hate the bitter memory that was the shadow of his father. But then he was too young to listen, afterbirth clogging his ears. What was she running from? What forced her to hide in the bottom of a liquor bottle?

Her look told him that she had nothing to say on the subject. Her eyes hardened, and the smile was gone. He knew the look, and he dropped his head, staring at the plate of food and wanting to disappear into the floor, or worse, skitter back into his hole in Limbo like a frightened rabbit.

Maybe that was the one flaw in his character, the distortion that led to his confinement—his inability to understand how deeply rooted some people's pain could be. He dreamed that they changed, yet gave them nothing to help them through the painful withdrawal from narcotic tradition, stuporizing routine. Was he asking too much of himself and everyone else?

"Is the food all right?" she asked finally, retaking her seat across the table from him. "You're not eating."

"I guess I'm excited about being home." He forced a smile. "You know what I'd really like is a drink. Is there any more of that vodka left? It'll take the chill off."

"I've got a little bottle upstairs," she beamed.

"You eat as much as you want. I can reheat it, or fix you something else if you'd prefer."

She left him alone in the kitchen, and he listened to the sounds from outside while watching a baby cockroach scoot from under the refrigerator, feel around first in one direction then another, only to scoot back under the refrigerator when he stamped his foot on the floor.

He tried to picture his mother as she was when he left for the South. He didn't spend much time with her in those years, busy groping around for something, some place where he could "do his thing." He had done two years in the United States Army and somehow had avoided combat though he had spent six months in the war zone. Still, those who diagnosed his condition before committing him to Limbo, pointed to his service years as having some bearing on his illness. After the army he had tried jobs and school, unsuccessfully, finding an emptiness in both worlds that could not satisfy the terrible craving for meaningful action that churned in his chest, wracked his mind with questions, options, possibilities, obligations, and responsibilities, real and imagined. The first opportunity that held any significance for him was the southern Civil Rights Movement. He envied his southern brothers and sisters for having a very real struggle, a right-eous war, a black crusade, to give deeper meaning and purpose to their lives. And when he heard that the students of the "historically Negro" college in Briarville County were seeking volunteers to help register people of color, in answer to the freshly scripted voters rights legislation, he knew he had to join up with them and be a part of history in the making.

But he had expected the battle lines to be more clearly drawn, the enemy uniform white skin, their dress white flowing sheets and pointed hoods. He had forgotten to consider or, because of his zeal and idealism, wasn't prepared to consider the breadth and depth of the problems not only in the South but in the entire country. His memories were bittersweet like the blues.

When his mother returned he poured a drink from the half-pint bottle of vodka she placed on the table. He grimaced as the vodka bit into his throat and scalded his stomach. But the liquor soon warmed his spirits and loosened his tongue.

They talked and drank and his mother played Dinah Washington and Nancy Wilson albums that fit well with his mood and the gloom outside. They talked and he began to feel comfortable, at home, confident, and free for the first time in a decade. They talked and laughed and he nibbled at his now cold breakfast until his plate and small bottle of vodka were both empty. But when his mother told him that she had planned a homecoming celebration for him that evening, he became agitated. He wanted another drink.

"Do we have to have it?" he asked, unnerved by the thought of mingling with and being spotlighted by people who, though related, were now strangers to him. Had they changed? Would they accept the changes in him?

"Butch asks about you all the time."

"I thought I'd just kind of lay around, you know, until I could figure out what I'm going to do with myself."

"It'll just be for tonight. And everybody wants to see you. You've been away for such a long time."

There was a knock at the kitchen door before he could answer her, and a woman called, "Mama Joyce, it's me, Debra Jean." She rapped again at the door.

"You'll like her," his mother said, and she got up and opened the door.

He was nervous. Fidgeting like a cornered mouse, he stood and manufactured a meager smile. The vodka helped. But the walls seemed to close in around him.

"Come in, Debra Jean," his mother bubbled. *"He's* home."

And he looked for a place to go, away from the spotlight, from undue attention. He put his empty glass to his mouth and knew he would have to have another drink, a series of drinks if he was to make it through the day and the evening's "family reunion."

His mother talked rapidly. Everything she said was about him. His skin crawled, itched, and he wanted to run but didn't.

A quick exchange of pleasantries and introductions did not ease the tension that gripped him like a high fever. He avoided Debra Jean's dark brown, bubbly eyes but could not help but be drawn to her ample hips, round, giggling mounds under the silky material of the rust-colored dress. Her tan leather jacket could not hide the seductive cleavage of her breasts, a valley between the warm brown hills, and he let his eyes play over them, fondle them lustfully.

Hot flashes sizzled over his body and, swelling at his groin, forced him to the sink where he swallowed down a glassful of cold tap water. When he closed his eyes he saw Debra Jean nude, the dark brown nipples of her firm breasts like great willing eyes, the triangular patch of curly black hair between her thighs screaming *woman,* and he thought, *The blacker the berry the sweeter the juice.* How sweet and hot was Debra Jean? He stole a look at her and was surprised to see her smile back. Did she know what he was thinking? That he *wanted* her, needed her, would take her right there in the kitchen with the gray gloom filtering through the window like a somber-faced voyeur. How long had it been, ten years?

Her perfume was a drug that quickened his pulse. He held his breath against its vapors and leaned back against the sink, his hands covering the bulge at his crotch. He wanted her to leave while, at the same time, he knew he wanted her near.

"This is the day!" Debra Jean said excitedly and the nude in his mind dissolved, though the hot flashes persisted. "I'm really nervous," she bubbled.

"Debra Jean has a job interview this morning," his mother explained. "She's just finished a computer course."

He mumbled, "That's nice!" avoiding Debra Jean's inviting eyes, his own tracing the lines of her hips, the curve of her legs.

"Where are the kids?" his mother asked her.

"I dropped them off at Mrs. Jenkins's in unit seven hundred, " Debra Jean said and moved farther into the kitchen to stand near the sink.

"I would have watched them for you," his mother said. "You didn't have to pay a babysitter. That little check you get can't go very far."

"You've got company," she said. "You don't want those two wild Africans around today. I'm sure you and your son have a lot to talk about."

Did she have a husband too? Some of his interest waned, and he felt as if he had lost something very special and was mildly upset when his mother insisted that he walk Debra Jean to the bus stop as protection against roving gangs. "Let her husband walk her," he started to say but didn't and dutifully waited in the kitchen door as his mother got money from her purse for another bottle of vodka.

As he stood in the doorway he thought of the young tough with a big handgun. How many were out there, lurking behind the graffiti-covered buildings? Hadn't gangs become obsolete when revolutionary fervor raked the community like machine-gun fire? And hadn't the members, once thought to be "senselessly" violent, or symptomatic of racial inferiority, found justification for their so-called "militant revolutionaries" who celebrated their "outsideness" in dogmatic rhetoric, selectively pilfered, and too often misinterpreted, from the pages of works by scribes intent on elevating awareness rather than ego-stroking? What happened to the political and cultural solidarity that was founded in rare cultural jewels, family history discovered in a long hidden chest?

In the 1960s, when anger and hatred coursed through the streets of Los Angeles like lava from a long dormant volcano, many of them, the young and angry, the hopeful, the lost, gathered into too small, too hot living rooms, apartments, garages, storefronts, rapped, read blistering poetry that damned and celebrated, fired souls, and tongues flapped in righteous zeal. Long into the nights they plotted a collective future few could agree upon. They drank wine against the heat and smoked reefer to numb the nagging restlessness. They wore their souls like new skin and swaggered through streets they once limped, raised fists stirring the hot summer air.

Where was the solidarity? The brotherhood expressed in handshakes and closed-fist arm salutes? In the pages of the local black newspaper he had read that progress had opened doors, ending the need for "skinship groups and clubs"; integration and equality were "constitutionally guaranteed," cried the black press, and *blackness* was discarded for American "vines." He had hoped against all hope that the black press was right and that the suspicions that narrowed his eyes into piercing probes was a sign of his own illness.

And it was noted, in yearly celebrations, that the "Big Burn of '65" triggered a flood of dollars designed to smother the ghetto infernos, slumbering and smoldering in reach of white suburbia. Botany 500 replaced dashikis, Benzes nosed out Volkswagens, and upward mobility became the new battle cry. It was the sweeping conservatism that marked the end of struggle, the victory feast held prematurely while the enemy retrenched its forces, that drove him south where racism, openly supported by the signs of the time—WHITE ONLY and BLACK ONLY—symbolized high ground still to be taken. And when he sang "We Shall Overcome" in the wet heat of the South, a very real enemy was in mind.

They walked in stony silence, gingerly picking their way over ground carpeted with brightly colored shards of broken glass, cast-off toys, beer cans, empty cereal boxes, torn furniture—*artifacts of civilization!* he thought, and flinched as glass crunched noisily underfoot.

Disoriented, he stuffed his hands deeply into his pockets and scanned the faces of the green and tan boxes where dark faces glowered from an amazing number of broken windows.

"I'd sure like to have the window concession around here," he mumbled to no one in particular.

Walking next to him, her soft hip occasionally bumping against his leg, Debra Jean touched his arm and said, "I'm sorry. I didn't hear what you said."

"There's an awful lot of broken glass and boarded windows. Earthquake?"

"Kids!"

"That bad?"

"Only when they throw Molotov cocktails or *shoot* the windows out."

"That bad!"

"Otherwise I guess they're just kids with little else to do and no one around them with sense enough to stay on their cases and make them do right."

The Gardens seemed strangely active in the early morning drizzle. "A lot of people out," he said, more to clear the lump from his throat than to encourage conversation.

"Mother's Day," she said sourly and then, seeing the question in his eyes, added, "welfare check day. It's the first of the month, the day the government eagle flies over the Gardens."

"Oooh," he remembered and fingered the crisp bill in his pocket. He liked the metaphor she'd used and tried picturing a huge red-white-and-blue eagle hovering over the Gardens with welfare checks oozing from its feathered rump. He coughed to smother the laugh tickling his throat and curling lips, and then wiped at the perspiration that formed on his top lip.

"You shouldn't have come out without a jacket," she said.

"I like cold weather," he grumbled, a cold chill shivering his spine.

A long, low-slung car crept across the lawns and passed them, the driver's head sporting neat rows of pink hair rollers that were all that was visible, poking over the rim of the car door like an African Kilroy.

"It's payday for *daddies,* too," she said viciously. "Baby-making can be profitable."

He sensed her bitterness. The years of confinement had helped to scrape away some of the innocence that once was a protective membrane over his sensitivity. He sensed her bitterness, and it troubled him because he couldn't understand it.

"Like a bunch of maggots on a dead cat," she hissed.

He couldn't agree or disagree. He had nothing to add because he wasn't very sure of anything. He just didn't know anymore. The Gardens, the faces of the people, the cruel eyes, hard-set jaws, were all strange to him now. He could only quip, "You sound like a militant poet; thought they all flew east for the winter." What was Debra Jean's anchor?

Her tone softened, her eyes warmed over. "I'm sorry," she said, "but I'm growing sicker and sicker of black people every day that passes."

He wanted to ask about her feelings towards white people, and red people, and yellow people, and brown people. He want to ask if she was nauseated by all black people, by him because he was so-called "black." But he said nothing and silently eyed the women gathered around a late-model car parked on the lawn between the buildings just ahead. At the far end of the building a group of teenagers, clones of the baggy-pants gamblers, milled about under a dying tree. The telltale odor of marijuana floated in the chilly air. To his right an old woman, bundled in a plaid flannel robe, waddled like a hunched penguin from an apartment. She turned a kerchiefed head towards the dark, puffy clouds overhead and called back into the apartment. "Marvetta, bring me a bucket or one of them big cookin' pots out the kitchen."

A young woman in a soiled and faded house dress, a baby perched on a broad hip, joined the older woman on the porch, with: "What you gon' a do wit' a bucket in this rain?"

"I didn't ask you to bring the baby out here," the woman snorted and shot a hard look at the younger woman. "Take that baby back in the house and bring me something to catch some rainwater."

"Why?"

"It's fo' luck. It's good water when it rains on the first of the month down home."

"You ain't down home, grandma. This is Los Angeles, and if you put any of that polluted rain on your head all your hair is probably gonna fall out."

"Marvetta, you do like I tol' you. I don't want no mo' of yo' back sass. Ain't nothin' wrong with this water."

The younger woman disappeared into the apartment. He stared at the old woman until she noticed him. He smiled and her eyes narrowed into a suspicious glare.

He looked away quickly and stumbled over a broken doll that wheezed "Maaaama!" in a mournful mechanical voice. A pale green glass eye winked up at him from the doll's crushed head.

As they approached the women animatedly huddled around the late-model car parked on the lawn ahead of them, he started to veer off and find another path to the bus stop at Imperial and Central. But cars and people blocked all the exit routes and he was suddenly afraid.

"This way." Debra Jean touched his arm and tugged him in the direction of the women and the milling teenagers, her steps hurried now.

Unseen hands turned the volume up on radios and stereos, and a variety of music surged from the interior of the monotonous concrete-block row and crashed against the buildings like breakwater against a dike; rhythms clashed and banged over indecipherable lyrics that splintered into discordant ramblings.

He framed the women from the corners of his eyes and caught up with Debra Jean's brisk pace. They all seemed fidgety, expectant. What were they thinking about? He thought to speak, break the icy spell of paranoia that choked him, but he felt that even a grumbled "good mornin'" might be considered an invasion of their privacy. They were in different stages of undress, one in tight jeans and wearing a tight T-shirt over her bra-less breasts. Another stood with her arms folded at her chest, her legs protruding from under a brightly colored Hawaiian dress like rusty tent posts. And another leaned cross-legged against the car, a cigarette between her lips, and snapped her fingers to one of the beats thumping in the air. They seemed old, yet he couldn't be certain, their ages masked by unnatural lines in their faces.

The women became more animated as they passed. The two men in the car cast blank stares in their direction but said nothing, their expressions frozen as if cast in bronze.

They laughed as he and Debra Jean passed and one of the women barked at their backs. "Some bitches be thinkin' that they such a much. Think they pussies don't smell fonky as everybody else's."

"Girl, you crazy!" another woman chimed in.

And a third woman encouraged, "She ain't never said *that!* Go on and tell her 'bout her stuck-up ass!"

"Girl, you ought to be ashamed talkin' like that," yet another woman added.

He started to turn and look back, but Debra Jean, her fingers pinching into his arm, quickened the pace.

"I ain't got no reason to be shamed of nothin' I say or do. I do like I please, you understand. I'm a *project* woman. I was born and raised in the Gardens and my mama was born here too. I know what's what," she boasted loudly. "I get high when

I want to, and when I want me some sweet meat, I fuck who I want to and when I want to."

"You mean anyone you can fool into wanting to stick they thing off in your *grand canyon.*"

"I wouldn't take no shit like that," someone signified.

"Well, at least I don't blow up like no black blimp every time a man grab at my drawers."

"I ain't 'shamed of none of my chil'ren. And you can bet they all know who they daddies is."

"Bitch, what you tryin' to say? You got something to say 'bout my kids you better say somethin' nice."

"Don't call me no bitch!"

"What else is you?!"

Their voices trailed off behind him, lost in the music and the confusion of auto horns that added a mechanical dimension to the circus sound.

"Sure would like me a big piece of that," came from one of the teenagers near the dead tree.

Debra Jean hurried her steps and said, "Don't say anything. Don't even look at them. They're looking for trouble and they don't care who they give it to."

His legs trembled, his pulse raced. What had he come home to? A no-man's-land run by children with deep voices?

"Nigger, you can't handle nothin' like that. Takes a real man, *home,* to make a broad like that scream."

He stiffened his back against their laughter, which pummeled him. Debra Jean's fingers tightened around his arm.

"Don't!" she whispered. "Don't do or say anything. It doesn't matter. It's nothing worth getting *killed* over!"

They emerged from the Gardens on Imperial Highway and walked towards Central Avenue, one of the major arteries linking the South Central Los Angeles ghetto to downtown. A police cruiser slowed and inched along the curb behind them. Debra Jean's high-heel shoes clicked rhythmically over the dirty sidewalk. The police car pulled abreast of them and the two white policemen, crouched low in their seats, scowled up at them as he silently read the words, "Protect and Serve," emblazoned on the door of the car.

"Don't look at them," Debra Jean whispered and yanked at his arm. "They'll hassle you if you look at them too hard."

"Why?" he asked and suddenly wasn't sure that Debra Jean hadn't been infected by some paranoia. Still he breathed easier as the cruiser crept ahead of them.

"They don't have anything else to do," she said. "Good, bad, we all look alike to *them,* even to the *black* ones."

"Haven't been told that in a long time," he said.

"Where have you been?" she snapped, then her eyes went wide as if she had let a dark secret out of a locked box. She looked away.

They walked in silence, with him wondering what she knew about him. Did his mother tell her where he had been? Why else would she have stopped so quickly? And if she knew that he had spent the last ten years of his life in a mental institution, what did she think of him? He felt her hip brush against his leg and his stomach churned. Could he hope to *talk* to her? Get close to her?

A pre-teen on a small dirt bike peddled out of the alley just below Central Avenue, stopped, and studied the people in the parking lot of the liquor store. A urinating drunk leaned one hand high on the graffitied brick wall of the liquor store and mumbled drunkenly in a loud voice. The police cruiser slowed and made the corner, its occupants eyeing the drunk, who suddenly jerked around from the wall screaming in pain.

"Aiiiiieeee, shit!" the drunk bawled and dropped to his knees. "My dick's caught!"

"Uncatch it, fool!" laughed one of the men gathered around a bonfire in a fifty-gallon drum.

"Bet that hurts like hell!" one of the other men laughed.

All eyes were on the drunk. The police car slowed and stopped just beyond the bus stop, where a woman watched disapprovingly, her purse slung over her shoulder. "Nasty ol' fool!" the woman at the bus stop clucked.

"Somebody got to help me!" the drunk slobbered, rolling on the ground in pain.

"Man, yank the damn zipper down!"

"I'll lend you my knife and you can cut yo' little bitty dick off!"

On alternate beats the men at the barrel, the woman at the bus stop, the boy on the dirt bike, all cast nervous looks at the two white policemen.

"It hurts too bad to touch!" the drunk howled.

"You a damn fool if you think I'm gonna grab hold of your dick. You can lay there and die fo' all I care," a crony yelled.

Tired of the spectacle, the policemen in the cruiser headed down Central Avenue. The woman at the bus stop cut her eyes and then, with quick purposeful strides, covered the ground between herself and the agonized drunk, positioned her pocketbook under her arm, and pressed it against her body, saying, "Aw, hush, you drunk fool. You ain't gon' die!"

"Don't hurt me!" the drunk slurred and rolled half onto his back.

"Shut up!" the woman shot, freeing the drunk's limp manhood.

"Lemme buy you a taste, mama," the drunk called after her and then added brutally. "Yo' ugly ol' bitch, what do you want for nothin'."

The bus slid to the curb and the woman started for it, but then the boy on the dirt bike peddled up, snatched her purse from under her arm, and sped off into the maze of the Gardens apartments across the alley before the woman's scream exploded from her throat.

The sound of squealing tires heralded the return of the police cruiser, which backed into the parking lot and braked before the screeching woman. A second later the police car spun into the alley and roared after the bandit on the dirt bike.

"They'll never catch him," Debra Jean said and started running for the bus.

"Good luck," he called to her as she boarded the bus. "Keep the faith."

She smiled back at him and said, "I'll see you later. Stay out of trouble."

The bus groaned and snorted away from the curb and he was suddenly very alone, though the morning rush-hour traffic splashed through the intersection of Imperial Highway and Central Avenue and people carrying umbrellas sloshed by without a word or more than a noncommittal glare.

Behind him was the liquor store, the cursing woman, the laughing drunks warming themselves over the fire barrel and passing around a bottle of wine. The woman cursed the wino, the wino shouted back, charging her with "being a stupid black bitch!"

Across the street a sign over a glass-fronted fish market read: *"You buy, we fry."* Next door to it was a food-stamps center, and next to it a check-cashing business, broadcasting that all checks except personal checks would be cashed for a fee.

On the opposite side of the intersection he saw a stretch of the Los Angeles River, which coursed under the street and trickled even in the growing rain, a brackish ribbon of green water confined to a trench formed by concrete banks. He had played along the Los Angeles River, ripped and run among the cast-off automobile and truck tires, crates, and torn mattresses that smothered the cold gray banks. Was that his river? The river he must learn to ride if he was to survive?

He bought a fifth of vodka and cigarettes from the liquor store and was surprised to find the clerk and most of the merchandise protected by counter-top-to-ceiling sheets of bulletproof glass. He hurried back through the rain and was soaked to the skin by the time he retraced his steps through the tangle of buildings. Children everywhere. Running, yelling, they careened around corners on dirt bikes or darted across the now busy streets that wound through the Gardens. The adults stood in doorways or waited in windows or on lawns, and he could hear snatches of conversations echoing each other. He walked the gauntlet, buffeted by complaints.

"My check better not be late this time. Got my rent to pay. Them siddity bitches up there in that county office don't give a damn about the clients."

"I don't know how they expect me to feed all them damn kids the way they cut my check. And I got to buy Easter clothes for them kids out of the little money I get. They crazy up there in the welfare building if they think folks can live off the little they give up."

"You got that right, girl. High as food is, they talkin 'bout cuttin' my food stamps because I got this little job."

"I wouldn't tol' them nothin'."

"Well, if they cut my check again, I'm gonna quit that damn job. Don't make no sense to work every day and starve too!"

"Last month my worker lost them damn papers we got to turn in every month and I had to go down to that office and sit a whole day just to get things straight. Ain't nobody got time to be sitting around in no welfare building. Hell, who gonna watch these damn kids?"

"Them people at the housing office sent me a letter talkin' 'bout I got to pay they rent on the first of the month for the next six months or they gonna put me out. Now, what do they expect me to do wit' them six kids? Where we gonna go? That mailman better bring me my check today. If he don't I'm gonna drop all them kids off at the welfare office and let them see if they can feed them and clothe them and put a roof over they heads on what they gives me!"

"I put in a service request for my toilet and they ain't fixed it right yet. And they want they money on time like this is some kind of paradise. They ought to pay *us* to stay here."

"I got my car payment due and them people down at the housing office be playing games like ain't nobody supposed to have nothin' but them. I'm gonna make my car payment. They just gonna have to wait for they rent money."

"I ain't paying them they rent this month. At least not on the first. I got me some other plans. They'll just have to wait until I get my check on the fifteenth."

"My refrigerator ain't worked in a month."

"Roaches is taking over my apartment."

"Them damn gardeners and maintenance men be too busy chasing pussy to do they jobs."

"Don't nobody care about black folks. It's a white man's world!"

"And niggers ain't shit! Nigger think he can come 'round here on the first and fifteenth like it's *his* payday."

"Girl, you know you like riding in that nigger's fine new car! Only chance you ever get to get out of the projects is when you riding with him on the first and fifteenth. "

"Stay out of my business!"

"What kind of business you think you got that s'posed to be such a secret? Everybody in the projects know yo' business."

"Girl, lemme tell you, the last time my check was late, I went down to that welfare building and went off on everybody there. That's how you do that! Curse them siddity niggers out and you'll get what you want."

"There's a skinny little four-eyed nigger work down to the rent office that thinks he own these damn projects."

"Yeah, I know what you mean. He come tellin' me that I had better learn how to pay my rent on time because my rent record is bad."

"I called that bushy-headed nigger and was tellin' him what I thought of him and these projects, and he hung up on me!"

"I'd make him wait for his rent!"

"You'll probably have to. You know you gon' give all yours to that nigger of yours and he come by here."

"If I don' then I do. It's my check to do like I want with."

He listened for the blues, but the growl in their throats was something else. Anger? Frustration? The resentment of children who threw tantrums to have their own way?

When he walked into the apartment, his mother was busy in the kitchen. She hummed something up-tempo that he did not recognize.

"Why didn't you take a jacket with you?" she scolded.

"I'm okay," he said and set the bottle of vodka on the table, along with the copies of the so-called "white" daily and the local black press he had bought at the liquor store.

"You're going to catch a cold!" she said.

He poured vodka into a glass and swallowed down a mouthful of the clear liquid. A warming sensation swept over him and burned off the clammy feeling that tickled his flesh.

"Why don't you get out of those wet clothes and lay down for a while before the family starts dropping by. It's going to be a long night."

He started to offer another objection to the "family reunion" but relented. It was something she wanted, needed to brush away the memories of the circumstances surrounding his long absence. He owed her that much, and more.

"What do you think of Debra Jean?" his mother asked without turning away from the sink, where she busily washed a package of red beans in a large pot. "She's a smart girl. She need to get away from here. It's no place for a girl who wants to do something with her life."

"She seems nice," he muttered, failing at focusing on the headlines of the newspapers spread out before him on the table.

"She's had a few bad breaks."

She rambled on about Debra Jean and he half listened, more concerned with the anxiety that twitched his spine. She said something about how bad it had gotten in the Gardens. Teen gangs held everyone hostage in their concrete-block apartments. And only the bold, the foolhardy, or predators hazarded out into the Gardens after dark.

The headline of the black newspaper was startling, almost dramatic. "THE ANGEL OF DEATH HOVERS OVER THE BLACK COMMUNITY," it read, and he scanned the article, which recounted horror stories about teens gone violently mad because of the side-effects of PCP—a.k.a. "dust"—usage.

Some dust users stripped off their clothes and ran naked in traffic. Others gained superhuman strength and, according to the newspaper, were too often shot dead because police said they were unable to subdue them by any other means. "Angel dust is the scourge of the black community," read the article, which ended by condemning the "black community" for "allowing the deadly drug of PCP to be so widely used."

An awkwardly written front-page editorial seemed to suggest that the drug problem was somehow founded in the culture of the black community, ignoring evidence that the culture failed somehow to cope with new frustrations, economic and otherwise. He winced as the editorial went on to raise the question, "Why do blacks continue to kill blacks? And rob their own kind?"

A cold, angry feeling tingled him and he wanted to scream out, *"Because they're there!"* And he wondered if the writer of the editorial would somehow be appeased if young black gang-bangers and robbers would kill and rob more whites. Did the gravity of the crime depend solely on the skin color of the victim, even in the so-called "black community?" It seemed a reversal of the philosophy that justified brutality against blacks, allowing indiscriminate attacks across color lines. Where was the *American*?

He pushed the black newspaper away from him. So much was happening, had happened, but he found, even during the years of his confinement, when information of any kind was treasured, the black newspapers allowed only a narrow view, a myopic presentation, and he thought of the elephant and the blind men who, holding fanatically to their partial discoveries, were unable to define the whole. What part was the local black newspaper holding?

An odd headline in the white daily caught his

eye: "RABBIT ROUNDUP HITS 55,000."
He began to read:

*A mile-long line of farmers and their neigh-
bors marched through a hayfield in a freezing
snowstorm Thursday to flush out fifteen thousand crop-eating jackrabbits, drive them into
the corner of a field, and club them to death.*

The wild rabbits, the article stated, were responsible for destroying nearly ten-million-dollars-
worth of alfalfa and grain crops.

*The herded animals were clubbed to death by
about fifty people, including several children
under the age of ten.*

"Start them young, don't they?"
"Did you say something?" his mother asked and
wiped her hands on a dish towel.
"Just talking to myself," he said, then saw worry
flash in her brown eyes and added, "I mean, I was
reading aloud." It seemed to satisfy her, though a
trace of worry still fluttered in her eyes. She poured
a drink and stood over him.
"I missed you," she said softly. "Are you sure
that you're...?" She hesitated.
He asked, "Cured?" and then answered, "I'm
cured. And I don't have to take any tranquilizers or
check in with any head doctors." He started to tell
her that the whole thing was a cruel joke that had

backfired on him. He wanted to shout out that he had done time as a "political prisoner," a revolutionary plucked from battle by traitors in the ranks. He didn't because he had not as yet dismissed the possibility that he might have been the slightest bit disturbed, albeit for justifiable reasons given the conditions that ensnared them all in black and white boxes.

"I think I'll go up and stretch out on the bed for a little while," he said and pushed up from the table.

"Good, then I can finish all the cooking I have to do in peace."

"Don't go out of your way," he said, then added, "Mama Joyce."

"Everybody around here has started to calling me that," she said. "I feel like the den mother for a camp for wayward girls."

"And a rattlebrained son." He smiled.

She kissed him on the cheek and he could feel her lip trembling against the side of his face. He had hoped the homecoming would be less emotional, and to that point it had been; still he felt a tension that threatened his own tear ducts.

"Debra Jean is coming by tonight," she called after him.

From his bedroom window he watched well-dressed women strutting protectively like great mother hens before scurrying broods of youngsters carrying schoolbooks, umbrellas, and schoolbags, their faces shining like brightly polished copper. They passed through the gauntlet of complaints in passive silence, watchful eyes keeping track of children and alert to any danger that might present itself.

A yellow three-wheeled motorcycle popped and sputtered into the parking lot, and a man in a light green shirt and dark green pants dismounted and brushed absent-mindedly with a wide push broom at the rubble littering the lot. The slight rain had stopped, though dark clouds hovered overhead. The man with the broom cast a worried look at the sky, mounted his scooter, and then rode off along the narrow sidewalks that linked the Gardens like the pathways of a funhouse maze.

Still in his damp clothes, he lay down on the bed and finished off his drink. A clap of thunder sounded overhead, and he felt vulnerable, separated from the elements only by the pale green ceiling above him. He closed his eyes and tried to sleep.

THREE

MAN DOWN, IN THE LIMBO BOX

He lay on his back, eyes focused on the pale green expanse of the ceiling, and he thought of the women who made up the gauntlet of complaints and anger. In his absence the Gardens had withered, become overrun with vermin that sapped its vital juices, or maybe he had simply grown to the point where he was able to see what had been obvious to others before.

He thought of Debra Jean, her ripe fullness, and fondled her softness in his mind until hot flashes beaded his forehead with glistening jewels of perspiration. He pushed the thought of Debra Jean to the back of his mind, thinking that she couldn't be married, or even living with anyone, if she was on welfare. Did he still have a chance?

In the pale green of the ceiling he saw the faces

of southern women, strong, secretive, living behind eyes trained to hide what went on deep inside them, or even just below the surface. He remembered them as they were the day he was transported to Limbo to begin his period of indefinite confinement, which turned out to be a near fatal blow as opposed to the ruler-slap-to-the-palm that was supposedly negotiated on behalf of all the concerned citizens of Briarville County.

There wasn't much of a trial, more of a quick huddle between once opposing forces, and his freedom and sanity were bartered off in exchange for peace and progress, and the people from the historically colored college on the other side of Pike's River charged him with threatening the delicate balance of equality established by celebrated legislation. And friends and fellow students shunned him, sniggering Freudian quotes that neatly packaged him as a maniac who probably had difficulties in early toilet training. Who else would find meaning in destroying the private toilet facilities of the president of the historically colored college across the river—special facilities installed by Sears and Roebuck, Inc., and reserved for the use of the president and those special, read "WHITE," patrons who might visit the institution to see how their donations were being spent? And his admission of responsibility for the series of "accidents" that razed a number of white-only toilets throughout Briarville County had done little toward creating an aura of revolutionary purpose around his actions. Maybe he was crazy. And too, he was betrayed.

It rained on the day of his confinement, and he knew it was the weather that brought them out, a ripple at first, a few dark figures inching from the rows of weathered shacks, across the muddy ground to stand at the side of the road. Tentative, frightened eyes peered from the safety of doorways, eyeing the road where it curved around to meet the gravel stretch that ran through Little Briarville and to the city limits of Briarville proper, marked still by the warning sign that no one had bothered to take down when the bright new day arrived, though illegal according to the Constitution. And brush and weeds hid the sign from view and memory.

Arms locked at their waists, the southern women stood stoically watching their men, who, calloused hands dug deeply into the pockets of worn overalls, lumbered towards the road, mud slurping and grabbing at their heavy boots, rooting some in the gathering darkness, their eyes on the sky, then on the road.

No one spoke. They had all grown hoarse talking, shouting, marching, praying, accusing, arguing, and singing. They, at least many of them, had clasped hands together and been beaten as they marched the gauntlets that were a barrier to their freedom. There was blood on the ground. Their blood. And they, like the people from the historically colored college across the river and the people of Briarville proper wanted the long siege to be at an end and reluctantly accepted the conditions of the peace treaty drafted by northern "Great White Fathers."

Responsibility for transporting him to Limbo fell to two redneck deputies from the Briarville County Sheriff's Department. Paved Cotton Road was passable only by dinghy on the day of his confinement, because Pike's River swelled over the levees and spilled five feet of water on the paved stretch. The patrol car was forced to crunch over the gravel stretch of Little Cotton Road, to slog through the rain-muddied section of the Quarters. Shackled to the backseat of the patrol car, he could see the women standing just back from the road, their eyes on their men, and the men standing like solemn grave markers at the side of the road, their eyes watching the sky, measuring the rain.

As the car jolted along the road he craved for simplicity, something that would ease the confusion and explain what he had tried to do, something simple—a song, a chant, a rhyme with rhythm that would tickle dormant muscles into action. He could not find his voice and passed them by in silence.

When the patrol car slowed and pulled off of the road for the second time he prepared himself for another beating at the hands of the two deputies who passed the wet miles with sips from a bottle of white lightning. Rough hands clawed at him and jerked him from the backseat, his shackles clanging noisily. His feeble struggle was met and nullified with a solid blow to the groin, and a pained whimper slipped from his throat as he doubled over.

They dragged him to the pool of light formed on the muddy ground. He swallowed back his fear, thinking, "The time has come!" He was on his face when he heard the creak of well-oiled leather.

"Get him up on his knees!" one of the deputies snapped, his tone brutal, his breathing harsh and clipped.

It was his time. He searched his mind for a prayer. Nothing appropriate came to mind. *Our Father who art...*, flashed across his mind in bright neon explosions. It didn't fit. *Now I lay me down to sleep,* nudged
its way into his mind.

What was he praying for? A staying hand? Life? At what cost? He needed a warrior's god. There was no snap or bite in the Lord's Prayer, or any prayer readily available in his memory. He needed a god who would speak like rolling thunder, his finger hurling bolts of lightning at his enemies. He needed Reverend Henry Highland Garnet's God— the God who did not support fanatical cheek-turning.

They tugged him to his knees. The sharp edges of his shackles bit into his wrists. Never before had he felt his niggerness more, cut off from any saving hand. He closed his eyes against the sooty darkness and tried to force back the shame, guilt, and despair that came with helplessness.

"Now, you stay right there, nigger," a deputy laughed. "We'll tell you when to fall on your face."

A rough hand jarred his shoulder. He was beyond caring. He had struck out, and they had won. Life had lost much of its luster; still he clung tenaciously to it, searching for a way out. He stiffened his back, a weak gesture against the .45 pistol in the deputy's hand.

"We're going to play us a little game, nigger," a deputy chortled from the darkness. "I'm going to test my luck and you're going to be my spade in the hole," he laughed, a sucking snort that caught in his nasal passage. "I'm going to take these super-load forty-five slugs out of my *nigger* shooter, then spin the old cylinder and slip one of them back in the cylinder, and spin the ol' cylinder one more time, and around and around and around the ol' cylinder goes...."

His companion completed the ditty with, "And where she'll stop, only the devil'll know."

Their drunken laughter surrounded him, caged him, cut him off from escape and mocked what little courage he had left.

"I'm going to rub you on your woolly head, coon," a deputy croaked. "My daddy told me that rubbing a coon on the head is the best kind of luck you can get."

"Ain't no such thing," the other deputy countered. "You got to ride one of them big-assed black bitches for the *real* luck."

"I'm betting my ol' daddy was right. And this

nigger better hope that my old daddy was right. Because I'm betting that I can drop this hammer on this forty-five three times without splattering this nigger's brains all over the Delta."

Thick fingers brushed and raked over his matted hair like fat centipedes wearing hobnailed boots. He cringed but showed no other reaction.

"Shit! The nigger's got half of the mud in the state in his nappy head. I sure hope it doesn't have any effect on the luck factor. It would sure be hard on my pocketbook."

"It won't help the *nigger* none, either."

The cylinder of the .45 whirred and clicked, clacking to a stop with a jarring finality. He mouthed the Lord's Prayer, his facial muscles tight bands threatening to snap and explode his image into the night in a million fragments. He waited for the eruption, the sharp pain, and….

"Ready, nigger?" the deputy with the gun said, sucking his teeth.

Without any further warning the barrel of the big gun was jammed against his temple and the hammer clanged down, echoing like a large steel door slammed shut on a steel tunnel. The thump against his temple was not fatal. He sucked air between his teeth and said nothing. There was nothing to say, and there was nothing on the long list of last words found in soaps, melodramas, and shallowly conceived "B" movies that was worth saying.

"Ready, nigger? One down and two to go. Looks like our luck is doing okay."

Again the rough fingers in his hair, and then the eternity before the hammer of the gun slammed into place with a metallic clap.

"That's two. That's two! Get the money up!"

"You ain't won yet," the other deputy sniggered as if the owner of the secret to a cruel joke. "You scared, nigger?" he laughed. "Come on, nigger, bug them ol' eyes out and show us how scared you are, and maybe
I'll tell him to stop."

He heard them drinking, heard the sound of their boots on the muddy ground.

"What you think, nigger?" The deputy prodded his temple with the barrel of the gun. "You think you got enough luck left in your woolly head to take one more chance with this big forty-five of mine? Well, what d'ya think, nigger? Are you one of the unlucky ones?"

"Maybe he keeps all his luck to himself, or maybe he used it all up. How about it, coon? Don't you think you're lucky that you didn't pull your little number a few years ago when things were the way God intended them to be in the South? White man up, and the nigger where the white man tell him to be. A few years ago you'd be dancing like a big black roasting puppet from the biggest tree we could find."

He said nothing. There was no common ground on which they could meet and communicate. He saw that now more than anything else. No matter how he spoke, what he might say, how he might act, it all made little difference because *they* were not convinced that he had a right to feel or say anything. He felt the butt of a cruel joke played on him by "Great White Fathers" who scripted him a paper existence.

Words rushed through his head, once important words that raced now like denuded peacocks through his head, and he let them out, knowing that he could not die, be so abused without saying something, anything that would displease his *murderers*. If he could come back and haunt them he would, but he could only talk, parrot words that had never meant anything:

"A-all p-persons," he spluttered, his mouth dry, his lips cracked with dry blood, "born or naturalized in the United States and subject to the jurisdiction thereof…. "

"It's talking!"

"…are citizens of the United States…. "

"What's he saying?"

"…and of the State wherein they reside…."

"Commietripe, probably."

"…No state shall make or enforce any law which shall abridge…t-the p-privileges or i-immunities of citizens of the United States…. "

"Shut him up and let's get out of here. It's going to really start coming down in a little while."

"Come on, let's have a little more fun with the coon. You know we aren't going to get many more chances like this with all the talk about the New South and with them Federals ready to jump into a white man's business every time one of these coons gets a nosebleed."

"Coon." The deputy jammed the barrel of the gun against his temple. "Where's the en-double-ass-cee-pee? Huh? Where's ol' Reverend Rubberlip Coon? You think he's going to come riding out of hell in a red Cadillac filled with nigger-loving liberals and save your black ass from what I got in mind for you? You might as well put the watermelon back in the fridge, ain't nobody coming for dinner!"

They laughed, and he felt small. He had no quick-witted quip on the tip of his tongue. They had beaten most of the cockiness out of him. And no one was coming to help him. No white knight. No charging cavalry. No U.S. Marines. He wanted to stand, run, but couldn't muster the strength.

"You want to sing one of your coon songs?"

Why not? he thought. Why not a few rousing, soothing bars of "Lift Every Voice and Sing?"

"You know," a deputy drawled, "maybe it ain't such a good idea to go too far with this coon."

"You ain't turning chicken?"

"You're not really going to go through with this?"

"I said that I was. And you said you were in it with me."

"Naw! I never said that I was going to help you to...to kill the coon. I thought we was just going to mess him up a little, teach him a good lesson...."

"Nobody'll miss this one. He's crazy. Even coons got sense enough not to want crazy niggers hanging around and running loose."

"But he's not from down here. Don't you know that? When you deal with these northern niggers, you've got to be careful how you go about things."

"I'm telling you: even his own kind don't want this one. He's a troublemaker."

The deputy spat, and he felt spittle oozing down his face. He did not move.

"What's the matter, coon? Too scared to talk any more of that commie crap?"

He was incensed by his impotence. The rage ate away at his insides. A peal of thunder cracked the sticky silence, followed by a jagged bolt of yellow light. And he *was* scared. He wanted out. Dead he proved nothing. And from the back of his mind a tiny voice encouraged, *"Live, nigger. Shuffle for them. Don't you know how? You've seen it done enough times. Grin a little wider, scrape a little lower. Lay down a few choruses of 'Ol' Folks at Home.' What difference do it make, man? Dead ain't nothing at all!"*

He thought to stand, a smile masking the pain and the lie, and say, "Look'a here, white folks, I was only kidding. Didn't mean to do no harm. I *know* you the baddest cats in the jungle. Man, you *know* I don't want no *freedom;* give me good ol' care and security any time. I just didn't know what was happening, you know, monkey-see, monkey-got-to-do? And smoking them funny little ol' cigarettes didn't help!"

The lie wouldn't come out but it bottled up in

him and he lost control of his body, a warm trickle tickling his thigh.

"Look at the nigger! He's going spastic or something."

"Didn't figure the nigger would have an attack. Look at his eyes, bugging out like big marbles, like he's seen a ghost...."

"Or is *about* to see a ghost!"

"Bet he'll piss on himself, scared as he is!"

The tiny voice jeered from its perch at the back of his head: *"Malcolm didn't piss on himself! Nat Turner didn't piss on himself. Martin managed to hold his water!"* But where were *they* now?

"Come on, let's just whip the coon some more and take him on to the crazy house! That'll teach him good."

"I'm going through with what we planned. It's all up to the nigger. If his luck holds out, well, we'll do like you say. He's got one more chance." He paused, laughed. "You ready to die, nigger?"

The barrel of the .45 felt like white-hot iron against his forehead, branding him with the tag *coward*. And outrage surged up from his bowels, steamed up in his throat, and bulged his cheeks; his body jerked epileptically, and he screamed out, "Motherfuck you and your mammies!" and swung his body towards his persecutors.

A blistering explosion erupted near his right ear and bright flashes of light streaked and exploded in his head, and there was a sudden moment of excruciating pain until a warm blackness dragged him under its bubbly surface and there was nothing until....

"Kick him in the ass! If he's alive, he'll squeal some."

He stiffened against the heavy blow that landed on cue just below the small of his back. The muddy boot glanced off the soft muscles of his butt and thudded solidly against the wood floor. He fought back the *squeal* tickling his throat and was surprised himself to find that he was still alive, or at least still in transit to the golden gates of the Promised Land.

"Should'a left the nigger back in the woods."

"What I am trying to say," the whiner spat, his tone showing his irritation, "is that we are completing studies and extensive work that will further explain in scientific terms why the kneeegra is inferior to the white race. We know that it is a fact of his birth, even more, the will of God. But we haven't found the precise combination of ingredients, unique to the kneeegra, that is responsible. Once we find that element wc will better be able to find ways of altering the kneeegra's natural leanings towards violence, sexual promiscuity, and other anti-social acts. I am a doctoral student, and my thesis involves an evaluation of the kneeegra's sexual behavior."

A chain scraped against the hardwood floors. Precise footsteps squeaked, and heavy boots shuffled and scratched. He sensed a presence over him.

"He looks in pretty bad shape."

The student knelt on one knee beside him. His white smock was a drab yellow in the subdued light. He smelled of medicine and mint. The student placed clammy fingers at his pulse. He clenched his teeth, biting down hard on his already bloodied lips.

"Well?" a deputy asked.

"He's got a strong pulse," the student said, smacking his lips.

"Okay, you got the nigger, and all we need is a signature on this paper saying we delivered him to you in one piece."

"I don't know."

"Come on, sign the papers. We've got a long drive back to Briarville, and the way the rain is coming down, the roads may not be there."

"Give me the papers," the student said finally. "I see that I'll never get anything done if I stand here and argue with you all night."

"Here you go. Sign right there at the bottom of that one and in the middle of that one."

"The next one you bring, I hope you bring in better condition. There are people who are beginning to frown on this kind of treatment of the kneeegra."

"Aaaaaaaaaaaaaaaarrrrrrrrrgggghhhhhhhh!"

"What the hell was *that?*" a deputy demanded.

"Sign these papers so we can get the hell out of here," his partner shot.

"Aaaaaaaaaaaaaaaarrrrrrrrrgggghhhhhhhh!"

It was a heavy, urgent wail that exploded from the bowels of the building, hovered over them, between them and the storm raging outside, and

126

froze them in time.

"Did you hear that?" the deputy asked. "Did you hear that, that...?"

"I ain't deaf. I heard it."

"Sounds like they killing somebody back there."

The wail faded into the storm and then there was only the dull swipe of the overhead fan and the sound of heavy breathing. Did they really apply electric power to exposed brain tissue? He was near panic, his eyes wide saucers, his ears groping for every sound.

The rain pounded steadily just outside the building. By gently moving his head he found that he had a good view of the front entrance to Limbo. The big double doors were hurled open against the steamy heat, double screen doors protecting the opening against the invasion of insects that massed and swarmed under the bare bulb bathing the front steps in a yellow glow.

"It's just one of the inmates," the student explained.

"What did you say you were studying?" asked one of the deputies from his place near the double doors.

"The kneegra's sexual behavior," the student said, still standing over him.

"Sounds like somebody's *yanking* on his thing!" a deputy said.

"Come on, let's go," his partner encouraged. "It's creepy here." He paused. "I mean real *spooky*. Let's get out of here."

"There's really nothing to be afraid of," the student offered. "We keep the dangerous ones under sedation. They are no trouble at all. Just like children." He paused, then said slowly, "Bring him back to the intake room and I'll sign your papers."

His senses were fully awake. The pain that numbed his nerve endings was now a very real threat. He flinched at each stinging stab and wanted to scream but was shocked to find that he could not control his jaw.

He sniffed air into his lungs. It was tainted by the heady scent of an overly sweet cologne that did not mask the antiseptic smell permeating the student's crisp yet drab clothes. He was nauseous and gagged, a feeble, rasping croak.

"The intake room is right down the hall," the student said. "You'll have to carry him. The director is very particular about these floors. This is a hospital."

"Come on," a deputy snapped. "Let's drop the coon in the back room and find us a drink."

"Sure."

Rough hands jostled him. Strong fingers wound into the fabric of his overalls. His eyes wide, unblinking, he stared blankly ahead as the deputy shuffled over and bent down before him. Their eyes met. He froze the deputy momentarily with his glassy stare. The spell was promptly broken when the other deputy tugged violently at the strap of his overalls, jerking his head back. The deputy looked away. It was a small victory for him in a war where none were to be expected.

"Where do you want the nigger?"

"Back this way," the student said.

He felt himself being lifted and closed his eyes. He prayed for the power to climb out of the battered shell that was his body. Let them have it, he thought. He only wanted to escape the pain. Escape its burdensome reality.

He could control some of the chaos in his mind but it, combined with the pain that raked his body, was becoming more than he could handle. If only he could separate his essence from his flesh. Without support, a cheering section, someone to mourn, someone to gain—other than the enemy—it all seemed a terrible waste.

Crippled by pain, uncertainty—defeat—he could only wonder if everyone had been right, especially those who pressed against agitation and those who pressed for patience.

The hallway was a dimly lighted tunnel that bore into the interior of the building. The walls were drab and dingy, in keeping with the atmosphere of the place. The odors were heavier and more acrid the farther they went. The stench of stale urine seemed to ooze from unseen spigots. He held his breath against the thick, unyielding stink of human waste. He couldn't block it out and was suddenly conscious of—and irritated by—his own heady ripeness.

"Damn," someone said. "Smells like an open shithouse!"

"Ooooooooooooowwwwwwwweeeeeee!"

A long, plaintive moan, it seemed to ooze from the walls and, like bitter, thick molasses, it folded over them and held them fast in its sticky embrace. The procession stopped short.

"W-wha…?" was all a deputy could manage.

He felt himself slipping from their grasp. One of the deputies balanced his upper torso on his knees and stood stock still, the deputy's fingers grappling with the cloth of his overalls.

"Just one of the inmates," the student said after a long uneasy pause. He laughed a girlish giggle and said, "Don't tell me that big, bad deputies are afraid of a few crazy coons?"

"Watch your mouth!" the deputy blustered.

The shriek resounded throughout the hallway, which amplified it. It was suddenly joined by a chorus of moans and groans that seemed to fall into a rhythmic pattern. It was strangely familiar. The menagerie of sound flitted, swooped, and soared, rebounding off the inner skin of the asylum.

"Don't drop him," the student cautioned quickly. "Watch out for the floor." He paused, then said, "And don't drag your muddy boots."

The caution was met with aggravated scraping noises that did not blend with the heavier moans. The deputies grunted and managed better holds on his limp form. He did nothing to resist or assist.

"Oooooooooooooooooooweeeeeeeee!" shook the gloom, leading the chorus of moans and groans to the unseen rafters, where they taunted, jeered,

laughed, and cursed, kicking up a strange chant that ricocheted off the walls.

The uproar had taken on a pulsating cadence, like a huge heart pumping out sounds calliope-fashion. He felt strange, as if some important part of him was being peeled away like a skin being stripped with a boning knife. His mind seemed to float out and up, stumbling momentarily before catching hold of the tail of the mournful lyric.

With his eyes tightly shut he could see himself, a member of the chorus, looking down from the rafters at the figures in the dimly lighted hall of the asylum.

It was difficult to see where they began or ended, their shadowy forms blending into each other, absorbing each other. But no! Not *they*—them! He was still very much a part of the tragedy, even though he had learned to close his eyes and feeling to it. They were linked together—stuck to and with each other in an illicit embrace. They could segregate but they could not be separated.

A coarse voice broke out into a mellow blues. A guitar twanged sharply from somewhere. The moans subsided.

Woke up this mawnin'.
Tar was runnin' all 'round my bed.
Woke up this mawnin', Lawd.
Tar was rushin' all 'round my bed.
I was struttin' and standin' still,
Felt like I was almos' dead.

Tar Babe, Tar Babe, Tar Babe,
Grinnin', struttin', and standin' still.
Tar Babe, Tar Babe, Tar Babe,
Grinnin', struttin', and standin' still.
Gon' have to sing me some blues this mawnin',
Even though it's against my will.

He was the Tar Babe. Each time his enemies struck out at him they reaffirmed their dependence on his existence, and they could not pull away. But what did it mean? Where would the realization take him? His mind was alive with pictures, images. He did not understand though they were familiar.

"Right this way," the student said. "I don't know how, but they always know when another one comes in. And they always kick up that kind of noise."

"Where's that room?" the deputy demanded.

The chorus stopped. Sour notes from a guitar floated on the thick, hot air. He was choking, once again a part of the pain. He opened his eyes.

"Right in here," the student said.

The deputies grunted and puffed under his weight. He wished for rocks to stuff into his pockets, a rebellious thought that did not ease any of the pain. A door creaked open and suddenly there was bright light as the student flicked an unseen switch just inside the room.

"Where you want him?" Jenkins grunted. His fingernails had torn through his worn shirt and were digging into his flesh. "This coon is heavy."

"Put him on the table."

He felt himself being hoisted onto a hospital table. A hooded light hung over the table. It was turned off. The light that filled the room came from a source somewhere in the ceiling.

"You got some cuffs?" the deputy asked. "We're gonna have to take our manacles with us. We use them a lot on niggers back in Briarville."

"Roll up his sleeve," he heard the student say but couldn't see him.

The deputies turned him onto his side so that he was facing a wall covered with thick padding. "Padded cell," he thought, surprised that such rooms actually existed outside of movies.

Shooting pains attacked his pain sensors. The shackles were opened and roughly snatched away. He felt relieved as the pain subsided and the shackles were removed. He wanted to thank them—thank someone. His rage blinded him.

He was still coiled in a tight ball, knees pressed against his stomach and chest, his calves pressed against trembling thighs. He did not uncoil even though the chains had been removed. The pain was gone but the chains were still a very real memory. The sickly sweet scent that seemed to exude from the student was thick in his swollen nostrils. "What you got there, doc?" He felt the clammy fingers on his arm.

"Just something to keep him quiet if he decides to wake up," the student said. He swabbed a spot on his arm with something soft and wet. "He'll be able to think but he won't be able to talk or move."

"They ought to feed that stuff to every nigger in the South," a deputy snorted.

He felt a tiny prick that stood out from more excruciating agony. The clammy hands were pulled away. There was only the sound of heavy breathing.

"That's that," the student finally broke the silence. "I'll just strap him to the table to make sure. When the aides clean him up I'll fit him for a camisole...."

"A what?"

"A straitjacket," the student said.

He stared blankly ahead as he was rolled over onto his back. He did not assist or resist as they straightened his legs and placed his arms at his sides. Straps were brought across his chest and pulled, tightly binding his arms to his sides. Another strap secured his legs. He could not leave. He could not participate and felt himself sinking away from his body and deeper into a whirlpool alive with sights and sounds.

The lights went out and the door creaked shut. He heard the lock clank into place and felt shut off from all life in the soundproofed and padded room.

The bittersweet lilt of the bluesy wail that had hailed his entry into the State Asylum for the Colored was still with him, an acrid aftertaste that he found palatable.

He was slipping down into the whirlpool; the

haunting face of a grinning tar babe with wide saucer eyes glared at him from the center of the vortex. He wanted to rush up to him and ask *why*.

Though his body was strapped down to the table, he seemed strangely free and mobile in the swirling madness that seemed to gain another dimension—smell. He was overwhelmed by the smell of people living too close for too long and the unexplainable smell of frying fish, seasoned by the sharp stench of hair fried by white-hot curling irons, recalled the smell of the Quarters. Or maybe it was the drug he had been given, playing tricks with his mind. What was real? What was drug-induced fantasy? He didn't know, and the silent room offered no yardstick for comparison.

He was surrounded by a deep and lonely silence, like he had imagined the murky depths of Pike's River to be on those dog days when he escaped to the levees to be alone with his thoughts, or with a willing coed from the historically colored college across the river. The only sounds were provided by the roar of blood coursing through his veins, the erratic thump of his heart, and the *tramp, tramp, tramp* of chaotic thoughts through his head. The padded walls of the cell pressed like heavy, thick mufflers against his ear, and he heard the rumbling vibrations of deep and almost total silence.

The tiny voice in the back of his mind mocked the bittersweet blues song that hailed his entrance into Limbo….

Tar Babe, Tar Babe...,
Grinnin', skinnin', and standin' still,
Gonna sing me some hard cold blues,
Got to break your devil's spell....

The darkness turned hot and spilled and splashed around him like scaulding tar poured from a pot-bottomed cauldron, and it hardened around him, encasing him like a paperweight souvenir.

Soon after his confinement he became overwhelmed by an accumulation of his own thoughts and body odors, the antiseptic muskiness of his padded cell, and a build-up in his system of drugs intended to make him less aggressive and more manageable. He fought them and they sedated him, restrained him with straitjackets and harnesses, and restricted him to the eight-foot-by-six-foot cell until he learned, a singular revelation given his state of mind, that the more he fought them, the keepers of Limbo, the more drugs and restraints they employed to keep him in line. By that time the drugs had sapped his ability to struggle and submerged him into a cocoon of silky silence where the walls wriggled and moved seductively, haunted by specters before which he cringed like a frightened child.

Asleep or awake, his memories were taunting reruns of his history, turned to failures by a tiny voice that raked his cocoon with accusations, indictments, badgering him with a 20-20 hindsight that heightened the paranoia created by the drugs. Still, the tiny voice was company, a confidant and signifier, and he engaged the vicious critic in verbal duels to keep his mind alert, only to have his actions misread as further symptoms of his mental illness. He protested the diagnosis and they injected him with tranquilizers and strapped him to his bed in an eight-by-six cell, with the tiny voice that wriggled, he figured, from a warp in his subconscious as his only companion and his most severe critic.

Said the satiric voice:

"Nigger, what you should have done was cop a strong plea. You should have gone with the flow. But naaaw, you had to stand your ground—remember Custer? Blue eyes and blonde hair didn't save his ass when the shit got bad. That should have told you that a cotton-headed spade sho' didn't have a chance facing no white Indians. What'd you get out of it? Huh? What'd you get out of tryin' to be supernigger swoopin' out the sky and whuppin' on the bad guys? I'll tell you what you got, you got two, count'em, TWO ass-whuppins, from two redneck crackers who would'a sold their mammies to a Russian to get a shot at a nigger's black ass. But naaaw, you had to run up there and stick your narrow ass in their faces, and now you sittin' up here wonderin' why they kicked it. Well, I hope you're satisfied. You got yourself a professional ass-whuppin' and some Limbo time. I guess, all things considered, that beats dangling from a tree limb and

dancing over fire. NIGGER, GIT HOT!!!! Ain't no
female action here in Limbo, Jack! You got that?
No womeeeen! I hope you got a good memory. And
just when it was gittin' good to you, too. You just
a rabbit without a tail now. I hope you're satisfied."

The drugs had a double impact on his body. They
kept him non-violent but also helped to ease the
pain of the beatings he had received and would
receive, making the long hours in restraint less
stressful. Sedated, he even enjoyed and anticipated
the scathing attacks from his alter-ego. They helped
to pass the hours that, when he was sedated, became
a distortion of time and space; and in the windowless room he lost track of light and dark, day and
night regulated by the wall switch that controlled
the overhead light. When it was switched on, it was
time to wake. When it was switched off, it was time
to sleep. The little voice did not recognize time; it
came when it felt the need and did not leave until
it had agitated his thoughts, like the plastic snow in
a water-filled paperweight depicting a wintry scene,
into swirling flecks that shimmered in the darkness.

"Remember Mary Elizabeth Jackson?" the little
voice slithered from its hiding place and asked.
"Big hipped and hot?"

Mary Elizabeth Jackson, though he had never
admitted it to himself or her, had a great deal to do
with his decision to remain in Briarville County
after that first summer ended. They had met during
the voter registration drive and together tramped the
dusty roads of Briarville County's outlying farm

138

districts where many of the county's darker citizens made their homes.

They both learned a great deal that humid summer, a great deal about Briarville County, its motley array of residents, and its peculiar code of ethics and behavior, which most recognized without any organized training and obeyed with sullen resentment. But they were driven by new energies vibrating through the South, a tidal wave of activity triggered by an Atlanta-born minister who balanced on the crest of the mighty wave, leading the way to new shores. But the great minister was toppled from the wave and, though it lost some of its power, the young, the idealistic, the angry who were demanding their due, who returned from the "undeclared war" expecting no less than total American citizenship, picked up the mantle of non-violence and wore it proudly during those early years after the minister's voice was silenced. There were victories, great and small: dark faces matriculated major all-white universities, earned jobs in once redneck-controlled police departments, ran for and were elected to political office by historically disenfranchised citizens, some voting for the first time in their lives.

But the struggle stagnated as dark faces became aggressive presences in a white society that had buckled under to legislation defining "the Negro" as free and equal but had not yet themselves *accepted* the Negro as an *equal*.

Still, that first summer was magic. He and Mary Elizabeth Jackson, who was the daughter of the dean of students of the historically colored college across Pike's River and had never ventured any farther than the gravel stretch that ran the length of Little Briarville and the well-manicured grounds surrounding the colored campus, scoured the backwoods of Briarville County and discovered life in the raw.

The backwoods were a great deal different from the Quarters wherein, on the immediate border of civilization, was developed a certain amount of independent thought and action, realized in angry assaults on the citizens of Little Briarville and of Briarville proper. The blues was spoken in the taverns, barbershops, and bedrooms of the Quarters, and its syrupy madness too often forced confrontations with the world beyond the Quarters, where retribution could be both swift and bloody.

In the backwoods he and Mary Elizabeth marveled at the almost childlike innocence of the people who, when the sun was white hot in the sky, sought the shade of rickety porches or windowless shacks, where dreams were torn from the pages of department-store catalogs and plastered on the walls. But he and Mary Elizabeth at the time were unable to see through the mask of innocence that was marred only by suspicious, downcast eyes, unable to look into the depths of the pain and hopelessness that boiled inside the people over the long hours of the wet-dry heat that only promised more dreary days in the future.

Over the years he realized that, for some of the

residents of Little Briarville, the vote of the back-woods Negro became a product for bartering for favors from the establishment that ruled Briarville County. But he was a Limbo man by then.

The children would meet them at dusty cross-roads and lead them to the shacks and shanties where parents and grandparents and cousins and brothers and sisters lived in abject poverty and wait-ed, waited through the long dry days for some way to end the drudgery so they might live, realize some of the dreams plastered on the unpainted walls of the shacks that perched on rickety stilt legs in recog-nition of the power of the river.

He and Mary Elizabeth spent exciting hours in the fields listening to tales spun by people who had to resort to their own resources for entertainment to pass the hot sleepless nights. There in one of the shacks they met and grew to love the toothless Amos Wilson, keeper of the small cemetery plot in a clearing surrounded by thick pines, where the peo-ple of the farm and wood country buried their dead.

Toothless Amos was the record keeper even though he couldn't write. It was Amos who kept the history of the field people, their lives, loves, hardships, storing tales of those who left the area under whatever circumstances. Amos was also the storyteller, a weaver of magic tales that lifted spir-its and taught values and history. When Pike's River rose and flooded Briarville County, covering the cemetery in the trees with over six feet of water, it was Amos who, after the flood waters receded, located and named each plot in the muddy terrain and restored the cemetery to a historical accuracy that no one in the area could argue against.

One hot evening as the setting sun played strange tricks with shadows on the dusty ground before the weathered one-room shack that was the home of the Haynes family, sharecroppers on the Miller farm, Toothless Amos ambled up and, as was his way, broke into a tale without any warning.

"Little Ray," Amos asked of the elder of the Haynes children, who had hopped a freight and spent a week in the state's capital, which had earned him the distinction of being considered a man-of-the-world, "what would you do if you was to come into a bag filled with money?"

"What wouldn't I do!" Little Ray said. "I'd live like ain't no black man ever lived. I'd build me a gold staircase to the moon and wouldn't spit in the direction of the South as long as I lived."

"I knowed this fella once," Amos started, taking on peculiar shape over his toothless gums, "nice fella as I recall, but he had one serious problem—he loved money more than anything else in life. By the time he was eight he had sold his dog, his sister's dolls, and probably would have sold the shack the family lived in if he had known someone who would have give a dollar-fifty for it. The boy loved money so much that he slep' with his money in a money belt that he never took off."

"Even when he went swimmin'?" a curious youngster asked, his eyes wide and shiny in the light from a lantern hanging on a nail in the wall of the shack.

"But with all that work," Amos went on, nodding to the little boy, "the boy still didn't have much money at all and he had ran out of things to sell, especially because he wouldn't spend his money on much of anything in the first place. He worked two jobs, and then weekends. He hustled pop bottles and even bought his food at one of them places that sell damaged goods and cans with they labels off. And because the can food was cheap he didn't care what he got, spinach, noodles, soup, it didn't matter none to him at all. And everything seemed to be going along jus' fine until the day he opened up a can of food he had bought in bulk and found out he had sixty cans of dog food, and him being too cheap to own a dog.

"After a time, the boy got to the place that he couldn't work like he was doing because his health was getting bad from too much work and too much bad food. By the time his thirtieth birthday rolled around, he had saved up enough money to put a downpayment on poverty. And he was mad."

Amos gummed down a piece of hot-water corn bread and swigged from a jug that always appeared when he did, then continued. "So, one day, without even realizin' what he was doin', bein' weak with hunger and all, the boy went into the bank to change some coins to foldin' money and robbed the bank. Jus' like that. Tol' them people to give him all the money he could carry. And then that boy ran like the devil hisself was on his tail. He ran clear out of town and deep into the pineywoods. And he hid in the woods and counted that money and counted that money until it was too dark to see the numbers on the bills. And then he got hungry!"

There was a wicked gleam in Amos's eyes. "He got hungry like he ain't never been before in his whole life, even when he had to eat that dog food. Now there was birds and berries and rabbits and other such good eatin' all around him. But him bein' a city boy he didn't recognize what was good eatin' like you children know how to do."

Amos drank and took a long pause while the rapt audience waited impatiently, the sounds of the night providing an appropriate score for the tale. And then he went on, as if he had never stopped.

"He stumbled around and went deeper and deeper and deeper into the woods. He was so deep in the woods and the woods was so thick that, for awhile, he couldn't see the moon in the sky. And then he come up on this big clearin' where there was a bunch of little shacks just like yours, and he went up to the first door feelin' like he was saved. He knocked and, when the man opened the door, the boy said, 'I'm hungry. And I'll pay you for something to eat.' Well, that man jus' looked at the boy kind of puzzled like. 'Money is no object!' the boy said and flashed some of that green foldin' stuff he had stuck down his shirt. 'What's money?' the man asked. 'Don't use nothin' like that 'round here,' he said. But the man said that he'd be glad

144

to invite him to stay to dinner and then show him a piece of land he could work and grow his own food. The boy said something nasty to the man, and the man tol' him he'd bes' to find him some berries and don't come back to that house no mo'. The boy tried every house in the neighborhood and everybody had the same answer. Wasn't a one of them interested in no money, but he could eat if he was willing to do a little work. The boy didn't want to hear nothing about no work and went deeper in the woods lookin' for a store. But he didn't find no store and word is that boy starved to death just a few feet away from the best eatin' berries in the whole South, his eyeballs all bugged out and his green money nothin' but a pile of paper dust at his feet."

Amos's storytelling visits lasted as long as the liquor and the food was available. On some nights, he confessed, it took him stops at three or four different shacks to "git fed and liquored properly." No one ever denied Amos, even when he was not in the mood to tell stories, which was seldom. It was rumored, and some would swear to the fact on Bibles, that Amos was actually a conjure man who possessed awesome powers that could be used for good or evil, depending on Amos's intent.

There were many *believers* in the outlying areas of Briarville County, and there were a few practitioners and believers in the Quarters. Voodoo came with the territory, and though it was no longer practiced as openly as it had once been, the religio/magic art was not lost.

On hot and dusty afternoons, he and Mary Elizabeth drank ice-cold Cokes from roadside stores under the glare of leathery-faced men with red necks and sullen, angry eyes. Too often, he was sure the stares had more to do with the way the material of Mary Elizabeth's white blouse clung to her bare breasts like a second skin. Never allowed to leave the house without wearing a bra, Mary Elizabeth obeyed until she reached the stretch of Little Cotton Road that turned to dirt, and there in the bushes she would slip out of the constraints of the cotton halter. He enjoyed those warm days of summer, and at day's end they swam naked in the cooling waters of Pike's River with red, purple, and orange sunsets the only witness.

Mary Elizabeth had great dreams and even greater responsibilities. It was expected that she not only succeed but excel. But when they were together, alone on the banks of Pike's River, the rigid nipples of her breasts burning against his bare chest, she admitted her fears that she might never fulfill the great plans her father had scripted for her. She enjoyed watching the lazy flow of the river as much as he, wondering where it went, the kinds of people who made their homes along its banks, the secrets it held under its silky brown surface. And he wondered what it would be like to build a raft and ride the river like Huck Finn and Tom Sawyer, bent on adventure rather than escape.

He plied her with questions about the South and

she probed him about life in the West, in Los Angeles, the sunshine city where there were no racial problems. And he tried to explain to her the peculiar form of freedom experienced by so-called "blacks" on the coast, of the great riot of '65 that quaked South Central Los Angeles, creating after-shocks felt and broadcast across the nation by live-action cameras, telling her about Americans who raised black fists in defiance, frustration, and despair, who threw bottles filled with gasoline, rocks, bricks, chunks of concrete, to signal a sup-posed New Day in race relations, or at least an end to urban peace. And though he talked of the entrenched racism that was masked by fickle smiles, he could not help but remember home as a paradise where a man could stand his ground to another man no matter their color—as long as they weren't mem-bers of any of the Southern California police agen-cies, with whom a confrontation could prove to be immediately and irrevocably fatal. He told her hor-ror stories of his own dealings with police in so-called "free territory," but they could not equal those that had become etched into the bloody his-tory of Briarville County.

"Why didn't your father move?" he asked her on a soft summer night, the moon's rays spotlighting the secrets of her body, the soft browns, faint reds and tans, and blacks of her skin taking on new and different seductive hues. "He's an educated man. He could have gotten a job at a college in the North or in the West."

"This is our home," she said, "his home. He never talks about Briarville in any other way. This is where he was born, where he went to school, where his parents were born. We too have a lot of tradition right here in Briarville. Sometimes it's hard to give that up."

"How does that make sense? What kind of tradition is worth keeping if it is steeped in racism, restrictions, even murder? I thought all blacks wanted to escape to the North, anywhere, away from the dreaded Klan, separate but unequal education and employment, *separate and unequal toilets*. He more than anyone around here had the means to escape."

"How can you escape from home?" She was upset, her eyes hard, pained. "This is his home, my home. How can you *escape* from home? You may leave home—to go on to better things. But when you run—when you run...." She searched for the right word and then stared at the dark river below, its ripples shining softly in the moonlight. "When you run, it's not a positive thing. How can it be? I've heard my father talk about the way it was when he was a younger man, long before I was born. A lot of his friends packed their belongings in hobo suitcases and hopped freights to the North, or walked the highways out of the South, leaving everything—home, family, friends—even culture."

"Weren't they the strong ones? Weren't they forced to leave because if they stayed they would have been killed for their outlooks and actions, because they challenged the racist system? Didn't they have to leave because they were a threat to the South's tragic tradition?"

"My father calls them refugees, whipped dogs looking for an easy life. Even the ones you called strong, the bad niggers, were as much of a threat to black people as they were to whites In fact they spent more of their time harming blacks than threatening whites. And then they left, having changed little or nothing, and too often leaving their families to explain or suffer for something they did and then ran from."

"What would their staying have accomplished?" he asked, fascinated by the way her breasts rose and fell when she talked animatedly. "Dead they're no good to their families."

"They aren't much good running away, either," she countered. "I know of very few who have sent for their families, or even come back for visits. But I guess you wouldn't understand. You weren't born in the South. It's different when you're born here and educated here. Your outlook on life is not the same as people, even black people, born elsewhere. When the men run it is left to women to raise their children, afraid of the day when they know they'll have to tell them who they are and what is expected of them if they would *live*—stay alive—to be an adult. And you've got to raise boys into men, beating the fight out of the more aggressive ones so that the white folks won't do worse to them for being nothing more than nature intended them to be—men! How do you teach a boy to be meek, submissive, nonviolent, and still be proud? You never could have survived very long in the South, not in the ol' days."

"And why not?"

"You don't know how to live, at least not in the South, especially not in Briarville. You're too angry, ready to charge headlong into windmills or hop freights like the bad nigger refugees when they've flexed too much muscle. What are *you* running from?"

The question was like a blow to the gut. It took away his breath; he turned away, to the river. "I'm not running from *anything!* Why would you say something like that? You know why I'm here. I'm here to help."

"Did your revolution of '65 solve all your problems at home? Is that why you're here, to show us backwoods country niggers how things are done? Remember, you may not be a refugee, a runner, but your parents or their parents were. Someone ran!" Her eyes narrowed into tight slits, her lips trembled. "We don't need that kind of help."

He didn't know how to answer her because suddenly he wasn't sure of himself. Had he run from one battle because it had gotten too complex, too difficult, and into a more simple fight, a fight that was already marked with a series of victory celebrations? What voice did he have at home? What role did he play in the struggle, and where was his continuing role? He had none.

"It's not so much that the riot of '65 ended the

struggle; it changed its direction. It's become a more individualistic thing, with people having to go out on their own and trying the doors that are now supposed to be open for them."

"And why aren't you home trying doors?"

"Because I'm here skinny-dipping with you," he quipped, hoping to break the icy wall forming between them.

"My father thinks you're a runner," she said and smiled. "That's why he's not all that fond of you. He sees you as a refugee who hasn't got the guts to make his stand where he is, no matter what it takes."

"Yeah, I know. And he also thinks that I'm a chocolate Don Quixote, instead of an embryonic Malcolm X or Du Bois, or Wright or Ellison."

"Sometimes you show more aggression than common sense."

"You don't complain." He smiled and reached for her, his way of ending the conversation that was raising serious doubts he was not prepared to face. "Sometimes you have to show a little aggression," he whispered into her ear.

"Violence?"

"It's the American way!"

"It's not yet the *southern* way!" she said and pushed him away.

When the summer ended he enrolled in the colored college across the river and took a job clerking in a department store in Briarville proper, which had been forced to hire from the darker ranks or be boycotted into bankruptcy. Somehow, he felt, the fire that destroyed the once white-only plumbing facilities might have helped to thaw their icy resistance.

He did the proper thing where Mary Elizabeth Jackson was concerned. He courted her and showed great regard for the somber lemonade parties on lazy Sunday afternoon, which gave Mr. Jackson, dean of the students of the colored college across the river, the opportunity to expound, informally he claimed, on the direction of racial progress and the need to know your enemy and your battlefield and not rush off into something you know little or nothing about, which often sounded very much like *Yankee Negro go home!*

Mr. Jackson was a well-dressed and well-mannered man, an intense man with high standards and the will to accomplish what he set out to. And one of his greater concerns, as was the concern of certain people in Briarville proper, was keeping troublemaking outsiders outside of the South.

Had he listened more closely to Mr. Jackson he might have avoided the web that snared him for Limbo. Or at least he might have gained the favor of Mr. Jackson rather than his wrath, a wrath which saw the delicate balance of the South threatened by too impulsive ideas, by a methodology needed for a much different struggle from the one that was taking place in the South.

He fluctuated between the gin mills in the Quarters—where people shouted defiance at an unhearing enemy, plotting, cursing, on guard while the enemy slept peacefully—and the campus of the colored college, avoiding the gravel strip along Little Cotton Road as much as possible. The people of the Quarters and of the back country were more familiar, in many respects, than any of the people of Little Briarville, where the Jacksons made their homes.

It was almost ten months after his confinement before he was allowed to mingle with the main body of patient/inmates at the State Asylum for the Mentally Ill. By that time he had grown to hate the sound of his own voice; and the voices, the odors, the presence of fellow patients became a bittersweet change, even from the hideous little voice that taunted him during his "period of adjustment" in the silky drug-induced cocoon.

He reveled for a time in new discoveries, meeting those who, like himself, had been set aside from the rest of society because they couldn't cope or be made to submit. Limbo was a so-called "stable environment," where change, if it came at all, was regulated like the day and night of his padded cell with the flip of a switch. Soon after his release a collective reclusiveness closed around him as he felt forced into lock step with the other inmates, who wailed and chanted and whispered the madness that had bought their ticket to Limbo. And it was in the day room, where the patient/inmates gathered and babbled and played games and killed hours, that he met the Reverend Nehemiah Pike, who for all his faults was the force that made the years ahead of him almost bearable.

Limbo, he discovered, was specially mandated to handle the most potentially dangerous of mental patients. It was a honeycomb of small eight-foot-by-six-foot cells, only a handful of them blessed with barred windows opening out onto the small plot of ground where white crosses marked the spaces of those who never left Limbo, or onto the electrified fence that separated the asylum grounds from the railroad tracks and the forests beyond them. Only the most passive were allowed rooms with windows; the others, like himself, who protested were wrapped in wet sheets, constrained by straitjackets, and drugged. And the sullen and resentful were recharged by electroconvulsive therapy, exposed to enough juice to light a hundred-watt light bulb. His aggression earned him a dance to the tune provided by electrodes applied to the sides of his head.

And even his aggression was misread as a sign of paranoia, schizophrenia.

"Monkey-see, monkey-do," a doctor said. "The only aggression they're capable of showing is physical, erratic. They do not act in response to any mental effort that might suggest that they are linked to some culture or civilization. They are primal mimics, even comedians in their childish approach to life. But there are the deviants, the troublemakers who take aggression to dangerous limits. These are the ones who we have to find a means of controlling or returning to an acceptable level where they are no longer a threat or a burden to society—theirs or ours!"

Waxen and pale, the faces he met in Limbo's day room were a horror show of contorted facial muscles. Glazed eyes peered suspiciously from behind droopy lids. Words, often unintelligible sounds, oozed, plopped, spittled from lips grotesquely misshapen by involuntary muscle spasms. It was a menagerie of sounds and people shuffling, heads down, living zombies who jerked, twitched, and fidgeted as their body muscles and nervous systems cavorted uncontrollably, a by-product, he learned, of prolonged drug usage.

Through the fog of his own drug-sponsored stupor came frightening specters, spastic convulsions in green robes that drove him deeper into his own cocoon for protection. And as they focused their attention on him, his paranoia increased and he shuffled deeply into the pockets of his green robe, jockeying for position, for space in a world of shifting bodies that, he found, orbited unerringly in their own space, only occasionally veering off course and onto collision course in a neighboring orbit. When that happened there was a chaotic domino effect that threw everyone out of orbit to careen against each other. It was then that the keepers came out of their chicken-wire-and-glass-enclosed outposts to rush among them in their crisp white uniforms like frenzied ice-cream men, distributing tranquilizers in large doses. And in short order, calm would be restored and the green-clad patient/inmates returned to their jerking, twitching orbits.

There was a definite "skinship" among the patient/inmates, though skin tones ran the spectrum from pale and ashen gray to coal black. He shuffled in place, out of synch with the others, his back to the wall near the door he had entered by. To cross the room, he felt, would be a journey through an unpredictable and epileptic gauntlet, and he was afraid.

To his left, on the west side of the building, were windows that were barred from the outside, which gave a panoramic view of the grounds as they stretched to the high cyclone fence. In the far corner of the room on a high perch, protected by a wire cage, a television squatted, its myopic glow controlled remotely by the keepers from their glass cages. There were card tables, lounge chairs, and a faded ping-pong table scattered throughout the room. Two wide-eyed men stood at opposite ends of the ping-pong table, maniacally giggling and taking turns chasing after errant serves. Others played cards and dominoes. Some stared at the television in blank amusement. And still others orbited in private circles, babbling, cursing under their breath, and spitting.

A man broke his orbit and walked briskly from the far side of the room, his slippers scrape-slapping over the scarred wood floors.

"Good day," he said cordially, his eyes bulging hideously from sunken sockets in his coal black face. "I need your help," he went on, brushing a nervous hand over the tight hair balls that were knotted together on his long sloping head. "I am in desperate trouble."

"I...I...," was all he could mutter in reply, finding that his words were like gooey masses of mush, his lips rubbery limp. The man was taller than he though slightly built. The bulging eyes seemed to have the ability to rotate completely in their sockets. He looked away, wanted to run, but could neither move nor speak clearly, and it angered him.

"You see," the man with the bulging eyes said, his businesslike demeanor mocked by a twitching left eyelid that fluttered like an awning in a stiff wind and a right arm that writhed at his side like a headless snake, "there's been a terrible mistake." He turned a watchful eye towards the keepers' glass booth and then, lowering his voice to a confidential whisper, said, his words wet with spittle, "I don't belong here. You see I'm not like you or the others." He scanned the room with a nervous glare. "They all know that I don't belong here. But they're all in on the conspiracy." He mopped his mouth with the back of his hand. "I've got enemies. They're responsible for my being here. They've conspired to keep me here with...with these people. And I don't *belong* here. I'm not like the others. *I'm white!*"

He stared at the coal-black face, the broad nose,

and the kinky hair and tried to inch away from what was obviously a crazy man.

"I see that you don't believe me," he said, his jaw set hard. "You're just like the others. You'll believe anything you see but nothing you hear. I'm white, I tell you. I'm not a…a…kneeegra like you and these others. Can't you see that? There's a conspiracy against me."

He was becoming more and more agitated. "They made me look like this. Look, look at this," he produced a black-and-white picture of a blond-haired man who had no resemblance to anyone in the room. "That's me! That's the way I looked before they did this to me."

"Th-th-thhheeeyy?" he managed, a yawn emitted from a deep cavern.

"They did this to me, changed me…, made me like you," he hissed viciously. "I tell you I'm not like you. You should be able to see that. You're a kneeegra. You know your own kind. Tell them. Tell them all that I'm not like you. I'm not a nigger! I'm not a nigger! I'm not a nigger!"

He slipped out of his fragile orbit. "I'm not one of you nasty, filthy, ugly, black devils, sons of the sinner Ham. I'm white! I'm white! And all of you here know that I'm white. You're in on the conspiracy. You're one of them, You're trying to take over the world by making decent white people look—and god forbid *smell*— like you filthy devils."

He wanted to run but couldn't. He wanted to

punch the coal-black face that spewed white hatred. But his arms were soggy noodles at his sides. And he longed for the world of his padded cell and the tiny voice.

"You should be shipped back to Africa!" the man with the coal-black face screamed. "You don't belong in my country. You're not white like me!" He stared at the picture. "This is me! I tell you, this is me!"

"Awwww right! Let's cut that out!" came from one of the white-clad keepers in the glass booth. "Don't force me to put all of you in restraints." A loud cackle and murmur erupted in response to the threat. "I'm tellin' y'all to shut up or I'll sedate every one of you black bastards and keep you that way until I think differently."

The roar settled down to a mild rumble. "And you, White Folks, git away from that new nut. He isn't bothering you. Take your crazy black ass back onto your side of the room."

"You're one of them," the man called "White Folks" cracked. "You're one of the conspiracy. But I'll get out. My people will come for me, and then I'm gonna lynch every one of you black mothers." With that he stuffed the faded picture back into the pocket of his robe and shuffled, scrape-slap, over the floor to a corner of the room where the words "WHITE ONLY" were scrawled in large black lettering on the pale green wall.

"White Folks is crazy! You'd better come over here with me before you get yourself into trouble."

He turned to face an older man, his hair a tuft of white cotton, his eyes intense and confident under bushy brows. "Ah…, I…," he stammered, pulling back from the man who held his arms in a vise-like grip. "Don't."

"Boy, you better come with me before you get into trouble," the old man said and tugged him out of his tiny orbit and across the room to a table where a Bible lay open. "Sit down," the old man said and then took a seat himself, closing the Bible and pulling it close to him. "Boy, I been watching you, and for a time there I didn't think you was gonna make it."

"Huuuuuuh!" his voice oozed from somewhere far off.

"I know you can't talk well now. But you don't worry about it. I'll teach you how to take care of yourself. You seem like you got a little sense even though you haven't been showing it lately. It was all I could do to convince these people to let you out of your cell. They figure that you're not only crazy but dangerous too. And you can't be both! You can be dangerous and they'll let you get away wit' a few things. You can be dangerous and they'll let you alone as long as you got the sense to stay in your own space. But when you crazy *and* dangerous, well, they got to protect theyselves they think, because they ain't sure what you might do. Boy, you got a lot to learn if you gonna come out of this. You got to know that a man got to make do with what's laid before him. He got to eat low sometimes if he gonna eat at all. And here, in Limbo, they ain't gonna let you be what you was or what you tryin' to be. They want you to be what they say you is—at least on the surface of things. And you got to understand what that means, because when it comes to dog-kickin' time and they say you the dog, on the surface of things it may seem like you due a kickin', but because you ain't the dog they say you is, under the surface of things where they can't see, you got a chance of gettin' out of being kicked like the rest of the dogs. Look for the signs. They're all around you. When you can recognize the signs, you'll know when the weather's gonna go bad and when the river's gonna rise. You'll know when to take to the high ground."

He understood some of what the old man said and felt a certain kinship, a familiarity that he couldn't put his finger on. He was certain that he had never met the man, though he had the same leathery, burnished brown skin of many of the men who had peopled the Quarters and the back country, yet his eyes were brighter, more intense. Still he was sure that he knew the old man.

"Boy, I'm gonna look out for you bes' I can 'til you can look out for yourself. You got to learn how to do to get your own way. And I'm gonna keep this special interest in you because I know that you got sent up here from my part of the country, Briarville County. And ah'm almos' sho' that they done done to you what they done to me. You ain't no crazier than I am." The old man's face cracked

161

in a broad smile. "Boy, my name is Reverend Nehemiah Pike. Ah'm the spiritual advisor here in Limbo."

It was Reverend Pike's guitar, he learned, that had heralded his arrival into Limbo those many months prior. The preacher from Briarville had led the haunting chorus in the bizarre *Tar Babe* song with his deep-throated rasp. It was Reverend Nehemiah Pike who knew all the secrets of Limbo, its twists and turns, its ragged and sharp edges, its pleasures and escape routes. And it was Reverend Pike who christened him "Rabbit," saying "a name don't mean nothin' until you've earned it. And when you're around crazy folks, folks who mean you harm, or white folks, don't never use your real name until you pick the time." And because Reverend Pike never addressed him by any other name, "Rabbit" stuck, identifying him among fellow patient/inmates and Limbo staff alike.

He didn't mind so much; in fact he found the nickname more comfortable than his own name, which, when used by keepers and doctors in a professional context, lost all family context and became another label identifying him as ill. He liked "Rabbit" and secretly thanked the old preacher for christening him anew, though he was never sure whether Pike knew what the new name had become in the hands of the keepers of Limbo.

He never discovered whether the wily old preacher's name really was Nehemiah Pike. For a time he was obsessed with finding out the preacher's true name and devised elaborate schemes and conversations designed to trick Reverend Pike into revealing his true identity, if in fact "Pike" was an alias. Nothing cracked through the preacher's tough defense, and he set about devising a plan that entailed sketching the layout of the asylum—pinpointing each room, each keeper, each file cabinet, each lab, while fashioning a key from a pilfered spoon to open the file cabinets containing patient/inmate history records.

The days melted into weeks, the weeks into months, the months into years. Seasons changed. But by the third year of his confinement he had lost interest in uncovering the mysteries of Reverend Nehemiah's past. He found it more intriguing to listen to the old man tell his own story, the way he felt it, embellishing it as he pleased. But he was grateful nonetheless for the distraction of the search, which shortened the hours and better enabled him to cope. Reverend Nehemiah Pike saved his life.

But there were other lives swirling around him, lost in the muddled minds of vegetating bodies that shuffled, scrape-slap, scrape-slap, scrape-slap, in a monotonous ritual.

Barney was an actor who had achieved some acclaim among his "skin-fellows" by playing the parts of natives and servants and drivers and slaves in some major motion pictures. He had always aspired to more, to meatier, more meaningful roles. But there was something about his eyes, they said—too much intensity, too much intelligence. A little too intimidating, and no matter how long he practiced he could not get them to buck and roll in their sockets. And then one day Barney went mad, they say, went mad on the set of a movie and screeched out that he was as good as anyone there, except for his eyes. His eyes kept him from working regularly, and he plucked them out and tossed them to the casting director. Barney spent his days before the bank of barred windows, his empty sockets hidden by dark glasses.

There was Harrison Kingman, who remained sedated and in constraints, his face a dark mask twisted by drugs. Kingman was dangerous. Everyone said that. He had killed his entire family—wife, two sons, and four daughters—fearing that his home was about to be attacked by the white-sheeted Klan and that his family might fall victim to a more brutal death. But the Klan never came, and Kingman sat in his shack for a full week waiting before he shouldered his shotgun and marched into town and shot the first white people he came across. The brutality of the massacre was cause for not lynching him, due to the sense of perverted logic of the presiding authorities.

And there was the self-proclaimed nigger-lover who spent his hours, when not under sedation or under the eye of his keepers, verbally assaulting White Folks because of his claim to whiteness.

"You ain't no blue-eyed devil, though you might want to be," he repeated, his face inches away from White Folks, who cowered in his white-only corner. "You're a nigger just like the rest of us. Black as the ace of spades. Black as coal. You a kinky-headed, big-lipped, watermelon-lovin' nigger. But I love you even though you want to be white. Because I'm a nigger-lover! I love 'em jet black and warm cocoa, ebony and mahogany, persimmon-colored and peach-hued, tan and sassy brown, buttermilk and coffee with milk. Niggers! They God's gift to the world. Niggers! Cuddle one. Be friends with one. The Nigger is the greatest thing on earth."

Generally a struggle for space would break out between the nigger-lover and White Folks, which would escalate quickly into a loud bickering and pushing and shoving among the rest of the patient/inmates, put down only by the charge of the keepers armed with hypodermic needles and tran-quilizers.

The most dangerous of them all was Henry Turner, who was allowed from his cell only when shackled hand and foot. Turner spoke to God, a black god, a warrior god. And that god spoke back and ordered Turner to kill as many white people as he could. Sparked by religious fervor, Henry Turner attempted to carry out the warrior god's mandate and dispatched three of the more brutal of the local rednecks in his area in that god's name. The white folks said he was crazy. They banished him to Limbo, where his ideas would become pablum. Better that than a martyr, a fiery beacon to rally round.

Reverend Pike took him under his wing, taught

him how to avoid taking the tranquilizers and how to outwit and get revenge against the keepers with a new game—"hide-a-snake," which forced them to check their bedclothes and lockers for snakes transplanted by patient/inmates as a way of beating the boredom.

FOUR

WHAT NEXT?

The rain had stopped. Tubes of glimmering sunlight spilled pools of light onto the foot of the bed in constant and eternal motion; specks of dust danced and swirled in the shafts of light.

The bedroom was uncomfortably humid. He shifted his body on the bed, cupped his hands at the back of his neck, and stared up at the green ceiling, wondering: *What next?*

He had spent the majority of his time in Limbo *surviving,* which gave him little time for plotting a future after Limbo. And now, with the sounds of "free" life bubbling, gurgling, screeching all around him, he knew he would have to make plans, moves, decisions of his own if he was to continue to survive. And a curious thought tickled him: *Survive for what?* He had survived Limbo, his eyes on the day, though uncertain, when he would be *free*. Now that he *was* free a restless aching churned his stomach. *What next?*

He was free to do as he pleased. No longer was his world controlled by the flick of a light switch—his eating habits, his bowel movements regulated to fit someone else's routine. But what did it mean? The great rush he had hoped to experience when released never came. All he felt was a nagging emptiness, as if he had not eaten in a great long time and his stomach was shrinking in on itself, consuming itself. What did he want to do? *What did he know how to do?*

A great part of his life he had spent immersed in his history, the history of so-called "black people," Negroes, African Americans, niggers, Niger River people, stretching back over the years and reaching from the blood-red clay of Georgia to the golden shores of Africa. He followed the course of their river, studied its twists and turns, its rapids and whirlpools, and he stirred the still waters of placid pools fed by the rapids and searched for more under the surface of the murky waters. And the silt in the waters swirled like the specks of dust captured in the tubes of pale beams now splashing pools of light onto the floor.

And he learned from the great sages who dotted the banks of the river, where their names were immortalized on the trunks of ancient oaks by young adventurers with pen knives. "Du Bois,

Wright, Garnett, Ellison, Hughes," he clicked their names off under his breath. But the war was over. They had *overcome!* Or so a great many cried out in the pages of *black* publications that tallied black firsts like crazed accountants. And if they had overcome, what of the warriors? The shell-shocked? The war weary prisoners of war? What of the *refugees?* Where was the progress?

From the window of the bedroom he took in the Gardens. It was an ant farm of activity. Women stood sentinel at their front doors and then started off purposefully in the direction of Central Avenue after the mailman passed. Children had free rein and barreled in and out of apartments while their mothers watched for the first sign of the mailman. Occasionally curses exploded from tight lips, to be softened by fitful laughter that had a forced and nervous quality to it, unlike the laughter that burst unpredictably from the patient/inmates of Limbo, who were privy to *very private* jokes. Even in Limbo there was much to laugh about. But at that moment he found little humor in the cruel joke that was the Gardens, though still feeling the twinge of his own doubts about his ability to *read the signs*.

As he stared down at the activity in the Gardens he thought less and less of the organized and purposeful activity of an ant farm and more of the thousands of roaches who scurried from the dark corners of the kitchen when the lights went out. And he saw in the faces of the women and the children something he did not see in the eyes of those who still struggled in the South. There was no struggle in their eyes, just anger, sullen resentment, and he felt a stranger, an "outsider" who could never be a part of their world again. He no longer fit. Over the years in Limbo, even he had grown or at least changed. But there was a stagnation around him now—*at home*—that he felt would suck him under if he remained. But where could he go?

He left the window and changed into a fresh shirt, a blue denim memory that had weathered the years in Limbo with him. Mary Elizabeth Jackson said he had *run*, was running then. But what else could he do? After Limbo, he knew that he couldn't stay *there*. Not in the South. Yet he didn't feel comfortable, or useful, at home. He felt his face growing long and angry like the faces that peered from over the rim of car doors or from windows and doorways all around him. What were they thinking? Were they tributaries looking for a river to be consumed by, a direction, a road map that would sweep them from the pale green and tan faces of their Gardens' caves and into real life *outside?* Did they hear Du Bois, Hughes, Malcolm, King, their voices resounding like oracles? He could not tell by their blank expressions and for the moment was too tired to care. He needed something to change the brooding spell that was being woven around him like a too-tight straitjacket, constricting his movement, hampering his breathing. A haircut, he thought. He would get a haircut.

His mother was busy in the kitchen when he got

downstairs. The house was alive with odors, frying chicken, a roast, simmering red beans. Nancy Wilson was asking, *"Guess who I saw today?"* from the speakers of the small record player in the living room. He stepped into the kitchen to meet the steady gaze of a woman who sat at the kitchen table nursing a glass of vodka. Only a single drink remained in the fifth bottle he had bought earlier.

"He sure is a cute one," the thin woman drawled. "Bet you ran them country girls crazy."

She might have been beautiful at one time, and maybe with some help she might still be beautiful, he thought, but right then her nut-brown skin glowed a warm red from drink and her eyes were pink and alive with bright red snakes. His mother turned away from the great black skillet, where hot grease bubbled and gurgled around golden brown chicken.

"Ruth," his mother said to the woman, who swallowed down a mouthful of vodka and belched, "this is my son. He's been working down south for the last…."

"You done tol' me enough about him so's I know him like I'd know one of my own niggers." She paused, leered at him, and added, "Weell, maybe not as good as I know one of my own niggers, not just yet."

He looked away from the gaunt woman, who seemed a sexless skeleton, someone dressed in sagging pants and a halter top who had nothing to hide.

"What's hap'nin', Ruth?" he muttered, nodded,

and then said to his mother, "I'm going to get a haircut. You want me to pick up anything for you?"

"You jus' v-visitin'," Ruth started, hiccoughed, and then managed, "or are you going to stay home?"

"I'll be around for a while," he said, anxious to get out of the hot kitchen, away from the red eyes that were like fingers exploring his body.

"Good," she blurted. "Me and you gonna have us some good times."

He forced a weak smile, "Need anything, Mom?" he asked. "I figure I'd go up to Mack's barbershop."

"Don't nobody git their hair cut at that nasty little place," Ruth smacked. "It ain't nothin' but a hangout for dirty ol' drunks. You ought to go up on a hundred and third street and get you a California curl, 'specially with that good hair you got." She stumbled to her feet and jabbed a palsied hand into his busy hair. "You sure got some good hair. Bet you can make some pretty babies."

You'll never know, he thought but said nothing. Sensing his mother's eyes on them, he cast a silent plea in her direction for assistance.

"I want you to run across to Mrs. Tucker's," his mother said. "She's cooking up some greens."

"Fannie Mae?" he asked, and pulled away from Ruth's fingers, which were now at the back of his neck toying with strands of his hair. "The old woman across the parking lot?"

"They should be ready by now," his mother said and then shot, in an even tone, "Ruth, sit down and finish your drink. He's got things to do and he

174

doesn't need to do any of them with you."

"What's a matter," Ruth burbled and fell back in her chair, "he too good for a project woman?"

"No one said that," his mother explained. "And you know better than to think anything like that about me or any of mine."

"He sure buddied up quick with Miss Debra Jean and her school-going ass," Ruth spat and emptied the contents of the vodka bottle into her glass. She slumped in her chair, an angry child, her eyes glaring into the clear liquid in her glass. "I bet he got used to them high-brown and shit-yellow women down there in them colored colleges. I saw how he buddied up with Miss Too-fine Debra Jean. And come pullin' away from me like I was gonna rape his narrow ass."

"I'm going over to Mrs. Tucker's," he cut in, afraid to stay longer for fear he would explode and say things that he did not need to say, at least not then. And too, she was right. He did find Debra Jean more attractive.

"Ruth," his mother said firmly, "if you're going to act like that, you can go on home and come back when you've slept it off."

"Ain't nothin' wrong wit' me, Mama Joyce," she said, her eyes downcast. "I didn't mean nothin' by what I said. But you know yourself that Debra Jean thinks she better than me just 'cause she been going to school."

"You could be going to school too," his mother scolded. "There are all kinds of programs you could be getting into. You're no older than Debra Jean."

"Who's gonna raise them kids?" Ruth snapped. "You know I ain't got time to be going to no school."

"I'll be right back," he said, feeling obligated to say something before he left.

"You think she's better than me, don't you?" Ruth asked.

He said nothing and walked out the front door, tingling under a barrage of angry, unintelligible words spewing from Ruth like the debris from a broken dam.

What had he done? Should he have allowed her to…to…to do whatever the hell she felt, because *she* felt like it? What was expected of him? And what was Ruth's problem? Her children? Her lack of education? Or was there something in the Gardens that hardened eyes, narrowed eyes and minds with suspicion.

As he crossed the parking lot to Fannie Mae Tucker's, he couldn't help but notice the amount of attention he was attracting. And he felt all the more the outsider, a novice who had not as yet proved himself worthy to wear the team colors.

He was breathing rapidly when he reached the cover of Fannie Mae Tucker's porch. The heady smell of cooking greens met him at the open front door, and he rapped lightly, calling, "Mrs. Tucker," through the screen.

"Jus'a minute," came from somewhere inside the apartment. "Jus'a minute."

Lighting a cigarette, he fought for control, for *space,* and shifted nervously on the concrete slab porch, feeling much like he had felt when he had emerged from the solitude of his cell and entered Limbo's day room for the first time.

"Mrs. Tucker," he coughed through the screen, a watchful eye on a figure tottering along the sidewalk towards him. "Mrs. Tucker," he called into the apartment.

"I ain't deaf, jus' old and slow," Mrs. Tucker panted and stood in the doorway peering through the screen that separated them.

"My mother sent me over to pick up…."

"I can see good as I want to," the old woman croaked in a dry voice. "I sees who you are. Come on in."

She stepped away from the screen and he reached for the handle just as a tottering figure reached a point directly in front of Mrs. Tucker's apartment.

"Hurry up and come on in," Mrs. Tucker urged. "No tellin' what *that one* might do."

He stepped into the hot interior of Mrs. Tucker's apartment and looked back to the young man who stood in icy silence on the walk just beyond the porch. His face was ashen, and dead eyes were sunk deeply in dark sockets. Spittle trickled from corners of his mouth, which sagged open like a broken gate. He was suddenly swept back to Limbo, to the faces of prisoner/inmates, their faces reconstructed by drugs.

"He smoke that stuff," Mrs. Tucker snorted.

"He's near 'bout grown and hasn't had a clear thought or bright look in them dead eyes since he was ten years old." She shook her head from side to side and glowered at the young man outside her door. "Git on way from my door," she ordered. "You know I don't 'low yo' kind to hang 'round my door."

The man with the ashen face and dead eyes moved his lips but no words came. His arms hung heavily at his sides; his head rolled clumsily on his neck.

"Dust?" he asked of Mrs. Tucker.

"That's what they be callin' that stuff sometimes," she said and ambled away from the door. "Don't know why call it 'angel dust' though, unless that's where it's s'posed to put you—up there wit' the angels."

He followed her to a kitchen, where large gray pots simmered on a small white stove. She checked the contents of each pot and then took a brown paper bag from a kitchen drawer and began unfolding it.

"Greens I'm cooking won't be ready for another half hour or so," she said. "You come back then." She pushed past him and he followed her back to the front porch. "But I want you to take some fresh greens home to your mother too."

"Yes'm," he mumbled, trying to remember if he had ever been in Fannie Mae Tucker's apartment before. She had lived there as long as he could remember, yet he knew little of her, and as he scanned the countless yellowing and browning pictures that cluttered her living room, he wondered what secrets she held locked under the silver tufts of hair springing from her head.

Fannie Mae Tucker tugged with thick, gnarled fingers at the big leaves of the collard green stalk. Her hands knew hard labor. She prattled as she filled the bag. "Folks steal my greens like they want to," said Fannie Mae Tucker. "Too lazy to grow they own. Too busy making babies or chasing after them no-count men who leave them with them babies like they souvenirs from a county fair, you know, like them little bitty turtles you get for a quarter." She turned to him. "The ones they paint up all pretty and put yo' name on it and things?"

He nodded that he understood, and she went back to pulling leaves from the stalk and continued. "Them little turtles like the little babies is cute enough souvenirs, you know, until they start gettin' to the place when they need more attention than some of these lazy things is willin' to give. They jus' can't flush them souvenir babies down the toilet like you can do wit' one of the little turtles when the cute has wore off."

She paused and then with great effort stooped and dug her strong fingers into the soft dirt around a scrawny plant. "A boy died right here at this spot," she said suddenly, her voice coarse, dry. "His blood soaked into the ground and he died. I remember when he was born. Lived right down at the apartment at t'other end of the building. Sometimes I'd let him run on down to the store for me. You know. It's got so bad I'm afraid to go out to church like I used to. But he used to run and do things for me, and I'd put a little change in his pocket so's he wouldn't have to do no stealing for no little money like some of these bad ones who don't care nothin' 'bout how hard folks be workin' for they little money."

She patted the dirt around the base of the plant, straightened the sturdy stick she had the plant tied to for support, and then struggled to her feet. "They shot him dead, standing right here on my porch. Some of them gang members jus' drove up and shot him dead and drove off jus' like didn't nothin' happen."

He sensed her anger, her frustration, and was sorry that he had not learned more about her.

"Plant jus' won't grow," she said. "Jus' won't do right no matter how hard I try. I even put down some of that miracle plant grow. But that little ol' scrawny thing won't do nothin' but what you see. If I take that stick away I'm afraid it'll jus' lay over and die."

He thanked her and took the bag of greens with the promise that he would be back in about an hour, promising also that he would watch himself and stay away from smoking that "stuff" that "be makin' all these kids around here, including they mamas, crazy as niggers can git."

Ruth was laughing out loud when he walked into his mother's kitchen. He placed the bag of greens on the table and did his best to avoid contact with Ruth's red eyes.

"Greens aren't ready yet," he said. "I'll pick them up when I get back from the barbershop."

"Still think you ought to get you a California curl," Ruth spluttered. "You sho' would be fine then."

"Next time," he smiled. "Need to get a little of this wool sheared off first."

"Take this money order down to the rent office," his mother said and handed him an envelope. "You know where to take it."

"Same place?"

"It's all filled out. Just drop it off."

"They gonna have to wait for they rent," Ruth said sourly. "My check's gonna be late. Worker come tellin' me they cut me off 'cause they didn't get them damn papers back on time. Like it was my fault or something. My sister was s'posed to drop them off."

"Ruth," his mother started, her voice showing her irritation, "you know what you have to do, so don't blame anyone else because you didn't feel like taking those papers down to the welfare office yourself. Those are your children. It's your responsibility to see that…."

"Well, what am I s'posed to do about them children until my check come? Tell me that."

The best you can! he felt like saying but didn't, not wanting to aggravate an already tense situation. Why did his mother waste her time with Ruth?

Were drinking partners that hard to come by? A twinge of guilt made him lower his eyes and he started out of the kitchen with, "I'll get another bottle on the way back."

"You know just what to say," Ruth bellowed and then laughed loudly to herself. "Mama Joyce, he sho' know the right thing to say."

The parking lot next door to the liquor store on Imperial Highway and Central Avenue was a confusion of people. He recognized the drunk he had seen earlier, now engaged in a heated debate over the crackling wood fire in the big black metal drum that was ringed by shifting, shuffling men whose eyes were constantly moving from one face to another to the alley where a crowd of motorcycle riders laughed and drank beer, to the street, the busy intersection where cars spun by in both directions.

Music blasted from the loudspeakers of the record shop adjacent to the liquor store. The barbershop was on the other side of the record shop. He stopped in front of the record shop, and the heady smell of burning incense rushed out to him. The interior of the small shop was packed with people, bodies gyrating to the heavy thump and cadence of the record bleating like a wake-me-bugle.

A young girl, maybe twelve or thirteen years old, danced from inside the record shop, a flat package clutched in her hand. He smiled when she looked in his direction, then started into the barbershop but she stopped him with: "What you think you lookin' at?" She propped a balled fist on her hip and struck a sassy pose. "You ain't got the kind of money it take to buy none of this young pussy, so's you might as well stop looking."

Why wasn't she in school? he thought, then noticed the teens and preteens who milled around the parking lot with the drunks and drinkers. Maybe it was a holiday.

The young girl snorted something else at him that was lost in the clamor of the traffic. Across the street people were queued up before the check-cashing place and the food-stamps center. Peddlers hawked brightly colored house dresses, gaudily framed paintings on black velvet of nude women with burnished brown skin and muscular warriors carrying spears, floral arrangements fashioned from fake feathers and plastic flowers, lamps and plaster statuettes painted a flat gold color. People exiting the check-cashing place made the rounds of the street-corner peddlers, checked the wares they displayed from the trunks and backseats of cars, fingered through the racks of dark blue designer jeans that lined the sidewalk, haggled with the unyielding merchants, and then made their purchases.

Two of the chairs were empty, and a balding man in a faded pink smock sat cross-legged in the chair nearest the window, staring blankly out at the street and the people-packed sidewalk. Near the back of the shop a group of five men huddled around four

183

men at a card table. When he pushed the door open and entered the shop he could see that the seated men were involved in an animated game of dominoes. A few of the standing men turned disinterested looks in his direction; the balding barber rubbed a heavy hand across his shining dome and grunted, "Help you?"

"Can I get a haircut?" he asked, feeling that he was somehow responsible for breaking a spell that had the barber spirited away from the dingy little shop, away from the men who laughed and cursed and drank at the back of the shop.

The barber yawned, flashing two gold-capped teeth, stretched, and then pointed to the empty chair next to him. "You the next man."

He took a seat on the cracked and peeling bright red leather cushion of the barber chair and stiffened against its icy back. The barber took his time draping a pale blue apron over him, his attention on the world outside the shop.

"Ain't seen you in here before," the barber grunted and then turned his back without waiting for an answer, picked up his clippers, and switched them on and then off. "You new in the neighborhood?" he asked when he returned to stand behind the chair.

"Been away," he grunted in reply, agitated by the howls erupting from the domino corner. The smell of sweet colognes, dead hair, cigars and cigarettes, and booze permeated the shop.

"Didn't git no haircuts while you was gone either," the barber mused aloud and raked a comb through the thick tangle of hair. "When's the last time you had a haircut?" he pressed.

"Been awhile," he mumbled, hoping that the barber would catch his subtle hint and recognize that he had nothing to say.

"It's good you came back," the barber quipped and then laughed in his throat. "How you want it cut?"

"Whatever's the style," he grumbled. "Doesn't matter. Just so's it looks neat."

"Well, you won't have no problem about it looking nice and neat. I know my business, even though I ain't puttin' all that chemical mess in people's hair 'cause they want to have the curly look instead of the kinky look they was born with." He laughed a short bark. "I don't know what's gotten into Negroes," he went on. "When I first started cuttin' hair back in Birmingham, a Negro would come in wit' his sons, you know, and I'd cut all they heads. And I'd cut them to fit they faces, you know, sort of a *personal* touch. You see, everybody's heads ain't shaped the same. You got some long-head Negroes, and then they's them needle-head Negroes, and those Negroes who got heads that slope forwards or backwards—even had a customer whose head sloped kind of sideways, but it wasn't natural. His wife tried to knock one side of his head off with a hot iron. And even Negroes' hair ain't the same. Some got long stringy hair. Some got the kind of hair that beads up in little tight balls like b.b.s for a toy gun. And there's the ones who got that wavy hair, kind of straight with a little curl to it—that *good* hair, like some folks like to call it. But they wrong—ain't no such thing as good hair or bad hair. No, not where I'm concerned. It's the haircut that makes the man look good, no matter what grade of hair he got. I know, I been cuttin' hair since before you were born. I seen every kind of Negro hair there is to see, and if you treat it right you ain't about to have any problems."

He paused, clicked the clippers on, then off again. "How you say you want it cut? You got a lot of hair here. Can do just about anything, unless you want all them chemicals on your head like they use so these Negroes can have curly, curly hair. I don't do that kind of work. Didn't fry, dye, or gas any of them Negroes' heads long time ago when that was the style either. Told all my customers that I was a *barber,* not no chemist or no hairdresser. I cuts hair. Lost me a few customers, but all the ones I kept still got they hair. They don't look like they walking around with they finger stuck in no electric socket like that big-time boxing promoter, what's his name?"

He was thoughtful for a moment, then laughed, "Don't matter, but you know who I mean. That's a man who didn't take care of what was his to take care of. Now you see what he looks like." He laughed again; the clippers buzzed to life, then went silent again. "It's a shame when a man got that kind of money and his head can't look no better than that. You keep them chemicals out of your head and you'll be lookin' good. And long as you keep comin' in here, I'm gonna make sure you *stay* lookin' good."

Buzzzzz, went the clippers. "Give you the same haircut every time, too. I know my job. Can tell who a person is just by rubbing them on the head. Lumps on the head is just like fingerprints sometimes."

"Gimme three more monkeys; ain't none of these be knowing how to dance!" There was a flurry of activity around the domino table. The round-faced man, his skin the color of strong coffee, slammed an ivory domino down on the table and then slid it into place at the end of a long line of dominoes. "Come on, what's takin' you so long to play," the round-faced man goaded the man seated to his left at the table. "Come on, play, nigger, before I have to call the police on yo' ass fo' holding up the game."

A few of the men laughed, most didn't; they had heard the line before, even used the line themselves, and they all knew that the standard punch line would be used again before the game was ended.

"Man down," the man to the left of the round-faced man croaked.

"Didn't hear you!" The round-faced man placed a cupped hand to his ear. "What's that you be tryin' to tell us? Did you say you got to pass?" He leaned towards the taller, leaner man, who wore a Dodger baseball cap perched on the side of his head. "Play or pass! That's the way the game goes."

"Okay, you got a good hand. It don't mean you got to run your damn mouth like you ain't never been down."

"Play or pass!"

The man pulled the lip of the baseball cap forward and then rapped the table with his knuckles. "I said, I pass!"

"Say it like you mean it," the round-faced man chortled and spun a domino face-down on the table. "This is the killer rock. This is the one that's gonna make all y'all fly away from this table like scared ducks."

"I'm down," said the man seated directly across the table from the round-faced man with the laughing eyes.

"Say *what?*" the round-faced man challenged.

"Man, you just dropped a lucky rock," came from across the table. "You ain't done nothin' so great. My man still got a play for yo' ass."

"Ain't nothin' lucky about the way I play. That rock knocked two monkeys out they trees. And what about you, you gonna belly up like the rest of them, or you got some smart play you ready to drop on me?"

"You know you got the last six," the last man at the table scowled, studying the table. "If I had a just one rock a bit ago, I'd a made you eat them sixes."

"Nigger, if you was a broad, you'd be a whore who give up the money every time a bone drop." The round-faced man spun his last domino, picked

188

it up, looked at it, and smiled, then placed it on the table in front of him and spun it with a practiced twisting movement of his fingers. "And if you was white, you'd probably be a faggot."

"Man, play the rock before you explode. The game ain't over 'til the last rock's down."

"When it go down, you'd best to start gettin' up," the round-faced man charged, then with a grand flourish picked up the spinning bone and slammed it into place on the table with a solid thunk, causing the other dominoes to scatter. "Gimme three more monkeys, these here can't dance," he yelped, then laughed broadly.

Men pushed away from the table. Chairs scraped noisily over the black-and-white tile floor, and the men who stood as rooting gallery took their turns at the contest table.

"Gimme a shake," the round-faced man beamed. "Won't take me long to knock these monkey-faced Negroes out they trees."

"Grab you something to fight with," a large man in a battered fishing cap shot. "You can't talk the game, you got to play it. Now, grab some bones."

The men raked their hands over the pile of ivory bones and sat silently as they studied their dominoes. The tall man in the baseball cap grabbed up a newspaper and plopped down onto the empty barber chair closest to the game table.

For a long moment there was only the sound of traffic, the muted rumble from the record shop's loudspeaker, the occasional scrape of a chair leg

189

against the tile floor, and the drone of the hair clippers.

"Say you been away?" the barber asked over the sound of the hair clippers. "Long as your hair is, it's for sure that you ain't been in jail or in the service."

"Down south," he grumbled, his neck aching slightly from the awkward position in which the barber forced him to hold his head. "Been away to school," he said, hoping the little lie would end rather than encourage further conversation. He couldn't tell everyone that he just got out of the crazy house.

"The South sure has changed, from what I hear," the barber said. "They say Negroes is really progressin'."

"You bet the South has changed," the man with the baseball cap roared from his chair. "All the redneck crackers have moved west!"

"I heard that," came from the table. "And I think all of them have been hired by the Los Angeles *Pohleece* Department."

"Who you tellin'?" The barber rested his clippers and joined in. "Ain't I just got stopped in my Cadillac by one of them young rednecked bastards, talkin' 'bout where'd you git this car?"

"You jivin'?" came from one of the men at the table. "They ain't still talkin' that shit to a nigger? Not after all these years."

"Don't know what they talkin' to no other niggers," the barber said, "but I can tell you jus' what they said to this one. And they was serious about *how* I got my car. Went all through the thing like I was runnin' drugs or something."

"You know a nigger ain't s'posed to drive no Cadillac," the round-faced man yelled from the table. "White folks have always been suspicious of niggers that be drivin' Cadillacs. Don't know why you keep buyin' 'em when you know what's gonna happen."

"I'm gonna keep buyin' 'em and drivin' 'em long as I got the money to make the payments and put gas in the thing. Got as much right to own one as the white man."

"But it ain't the white man who be gittin' stopped every time he put it on the road."

"A Buick is a better looking car anyway," another man added his bit. "Never did like them Cadillacs."

"Nigger, you ain't never been able to afford one," the barber retorted, "so what you think you got to say on the subject? You bad as them cracker pohleece. Don't want to see another nigger wit' nothin'."

"You lucky they didn't drag yo' ass out that Cadillac and choke you to death," said the man in the baseball cap. "I been following these newspaper stories about how they be strangling niggers to death with that…" He scanned the front page of the newspaper and read, "'bar arm control hold.' In the past seven years they say fifteen people have been snuffed out by the law."

"At least they ain't *shootin'* us no more," said a thin man in a felt hat.

"Now what kind of shit is that? Man, dead is dead, it don't matter how you git that way!"

"All I'm tryin' to tell you," the thin man defended, his eyebrows arching, his voice climbing higher on the decibel scale, "is that the pohleece got to do something to control some of you bad-actin' niggers."

"I hope one of them hairy-armed cops locks hold to yo' skinny neck and see how you like it," came from the man on the barber chair.

"Some of them niggers be usin' that dust," the lean man defended, his voice all the more shrill. "You never seen what one of them niggers acts like when he's on that stuff. It ain't pretty, I want to tell you. They git the strength of ten men. I know what I'm tellin' you. I had a nephew to go crazy behind that stuff. Come runnin' through the damn house cursin' and breakin' shit and tearin' at his clothes, talkin' about they was somebody dead buried in the backyard of his mama's house. I jumped on that young nigger and couldn't do nothin' wit' him."

"Nigger, you couldn't cut your way out of a pile of toilet paper with a straight razor," fired the round-faced man, who impatiently watched the empty table, the faces of his opponents, and the dominoes he held in his hands. "Who got the big six rock?" he asked. "Let's git this game going. I ain't got all day to sit around here beatin' you niggers."

One of the players slid the double-six domino onto the table and the game began as attention was diverted away from the thin man's high-pitched story.

The thin man turned to the man with the baseball cap. "I'm tellin' you, it took me and the neighbors to jus' hold him down. His eyes was all wild and he kept talkin' crazy about God and…."

"Ain't no God," a short man called, then slammed a domino onto the table with, "Play behind that rock if you can."

"Nigger, who told you that?" the barber snapped, and the clippers were silent again. "You always comin' up with some off-the-wall stuff that you done heard on the streets. Now, who told you they ain't no God?"

"I read it in the newspaper," the short thick-chested man replied flatly. "News is that Moses ain't parted no Red Sea or climbed up no mountain and got no Ten Commandments from God or nothing like that. It was in the papers."

"I heard the same thing on the six o'clock news," another player added, poised between playing a domino he held in his hand and studying the board. "Science proved that it wasn't a miracle that parted the seas and drowned the Pharoah's army, it was just a tidal wave. And that is a scientific fact."

"God works in mysterious ways, his wonders to perform," said the barber. "Now, you remember that, and I don't want to hear no more atheist talk in my shop."

"What you so hot about? You ain't been in no church since Mack got killed in the parking lot."

"A man don't have to run in and out of no restaurant to know that they serve food," the barber said glibly, and there was a subtle threat in his tone. "Now, I ain't got no more to say on that subject. And all y'all know I ain't fo' no religious arguments in my place. If you niggers want to lie and kill each other over something, don't make it on the Lord."

"G'on and cut that young brother's hair and stay out the conversation," someone laughed. "Much as you got to say about religion, you should have been a preacher instead of a barber."

The clippers buzzed to life. "You jus' remember what I tol' you."

"How you feel about *Mister Raygun?*" a voice came from the crowd.

"You know how I feel about that two-bit actor," the barber countered. "But one thing's for sure, he's gon' make a whole lot of niggers sit up and take notice, or they gon' git put out with the trash."

"You mean put out with the Mexicans," a player blustered.

"I ain't got nothin' against no Mexicans," the man with the baseball cap intervened. "They ain't no better off than us black folks. Long as the white man keep us at each other's throats he ain't got nothin' to worry about."

"Well, you tell that to the Mexicans. They the ones who think they white."

194

"Nigger, you'd pass for white if you could," the barber shot. "Knew a nigger jus' like you when I was home, but leastways he *looked* like a white man, jus' didn't *sound* like one. But he wanted to pass so bad he played like he couldn't talk at all. Far as I know the nigger's still walkin' around with a pencil and a tablet writing down everything he got to say." The barber paused, laughed under his breath, and then said, "Only problem with the nigger was, he couldn't write worth a damn either."

"You lyin' on the man."

"I wish I was lyin'. You know you niggers be sittin' around wishin' you was white, thinkin' 'bout what you would be into if you was white, lustin' after all the white women you think you'd be screwin' if you was white, dreamin' about the niggers you'd be steppin' on if you was white. But ain't none of you white, or ever gonna be white, and if something happened to make y'all black asses white-white as the president's, you'd still be sittin' on 'em wishin' you was somethin' else."

"You sure hard on a nigger today," the baseball-cap-wearer laughed. "You talkin' bad as a white man."

"Somebody need to talk some sense into some of you niggers. Makes me sick to hear niggers all the time complainin' about not havin' this or not havin' that and ain't ready to hit a lick on nobody's job. The Mexicans'll at least work, and they don't care how much they git paid either. But these niggers, 'specially the ones live off in them projects, they think the world got to pay the way for them jus' because they black. Ain't one of them ever had no for-real, ready-to-lynch-a-nigger-in-a-minute cracker to call them out they name, or tell them they can't walk on the sidewalk or nothin' like that. They even git they *free* money *delivered* right to they doors like they some kind of royalty."

"I heard 'bout this woman who shot her mailman because he didn't bring her welfare check on the first of the month."

"Did she kill him?"

"Wasn't because she wasn't tryin'."

"I ain't never gonna understand how some of these people be thinkin'. They'll spend thirty, forty, even fifty dollars to git their hair all curled up like some pimp, 'stead of gittin' a practical haircut so's they can go out and git a job of work. They ought to know ain't nobody want no pimp-lookin' nigger, or no Jesus-Christ nigger workin' for their company. You got to be presentable. All them beads and stuff hangin' in their heads and them cotton rows," *corn rows* someone corrected, "whatever, still looks like a plowed field to me."

"You jus' salty because you losin' business. It's your own fault. You won't keep up to date with the times and the styles. You jus' an ol'-fashioned nigger who ain' ready for change."

"I know what I'm talkin'," the barber shouted over the buzzing clippers. "I know that ain't nobody gon' give no job to no nigger that look like he tryin' to screw all the women on the job, or look like he too pretty to git his hands dirty."

A howl burst from the round-faced man at the table. "You niggers ain't got no wind with me. Shit, I can play me some bones."

"You play them jailhouse ones," a player shot.

"Bet he won't take his ass down to South Park with them old niggers. They'd run him out the park."

"You niggers ain't so young," the round-faced man said, a wide grin creaking across his face like a great toothy cavern. "I can play wit' anybody. Y'all jus' can't take the weight."

"G'on and play the rock and quit talkin'. You holdin' up the damn game."

"Somebody call the police, the nigger's holdin' up the damn game."

"If Jackie Robinson had put all that chemical mess in his head black folks still wouldn't be playing major-league baseball," the barber interjected above the chatter.

"Integrating baseball helped to kill off the Negro Leagues," the man in the Dodger cap offered knowingly, a hint of bitterness in his tone. "Jackie was great, but there were so many others who didn't get a chance at all."

"Who you tellin'?" the barber said. "Ain't I seen some of those Negro League teams play? I watched Satchel Paige pitch a no-hitter against an all-white major-league team. I wasn't no more than ten or eleven years old then. My daddy took me."

"How you figure you was ten years old when you

damn near seventy now?" the round-faced man roared, then slammed a domino on the table.

"I ain't but fifty-seven," the barber shouted back, his eyes narrow slits.

"I don't know if I could have took all the stuff that ol' Jackie had to take." The man in the baseball cap shook his head. "White people did everything but run him out of town on a rail wrapped in tar and feathers. I remember where they threw black cats out on the field and called him nigger and stuff like that. He had guts."

The barber clicked off his clippers and offered, "Base runners used to slide into second base with their spikes up when Jackie was on the bag. But Jackie took it. Didn't start no trouble. Just kept quiet and played the best damn baseball white folks had ever seen."

"He didn't do nothin'?" the lean man in the felt hat gasped. "He didn't fight back?"

"Nope," the barber stated. "He knew what he was doing. He knew that if he fought back…, well, put it this way, niggers didn't live long back in those days if they fought back at the wrong time. Besides, Jackie wanted to play baseball. He didn't come there to be no boxer. And he knew that, if he fought them players out there on the field, nary another nigger, including himself, would ever play in the major leagues again. That's what the white folks wanted, and he wasn't about to let them have their way if he could at all help it."

"I would'a…."

"You wouldn't have got the opportunity to play in the first place," the barber said angrily. "And if they let you on the field at all, you the kind of nigger that would have broke out in a *buck and wing* on the pitcher's mound if the white folks looked wrong at you."

"*Reggie Jackson* don't take no shit from nobody. He'll go off in them stands after them fools."

"Thanks to Jackie Robinson he got the chance!" said the barber, matter-of-factly. "Jackie Robinson, Paul Robeson—they all made it better for the niggers that come along behind them."

The conversations drifted from topic to topic, from sex to politics and back again, each man providing his share of information, real or fancied, and opinions became brickbats used to bludgeon the less aggressive, the less informed, or just the softer speaking, into reluctant agreement or sullen silence. The loudest voice set the pace and the tone of the mini-debates, too often deciding the outcome by sheer force of volume rather than sharpness of wit or the accuracy of the information on which the opinion was founded.

Soon the barber fell silent and the domino players became more intensely involved in their game. The slap of dominoes against the wooden table, the sharp scrape of chair legs over the tile floor, and the high-pitched drone of the hair clippers became a narcotic lullaby, and he dropped off to sleep only to be nudged awake by the barber, who brushed lightly at his face, the back of his neck, and then his clothes with a soft, long-haired hand broom.

The barber pushed a hand mirror towards him. "Take a look and tell me what you think."

He took the mirror, studied his image in its glassy surface, nodded a mute approval, and then uncoiled from the red leather barber chair, his numb legs buckling at the knees as his feet touched the black-and-white tile floor where his hair clippings were piled like cast-off ink-stained cotton balls.

"Legs asleep," the barber said and extended a steadying hand in his direction. "Happens to everybody. Just move around a little, get that blood circulating." He looked disapprovingly in the direction of the domino corner, then said, "Some of these niggers be sittin' around so long it's a wonder they whole bodies ain't gone to sleep for good."

He fought back a yawn, rubbed lazily at the after-effects of sleep, which were a gritty presence in his eyes, and then paid the barber with crumpled bills, motioning for him to keep the change as a tip. As he turned to leave the stuffy little shop, a slender man in a neatly pressed and tailored black suit, crisp white shirt, and red bow tie, leaned into the shop, balancing three pink-colored pie boxes on the palm of his hand.

"Got your fresh, ready-to-eat bean pies for you today, gentlemen," the man in black said pleasantly. Raindrops glistened on his closely cropped hair. "Come on, gentlemen, these are the best pies you can get. *Fresh today!*"

"Not today," the barber said evenly.

"How about you gentlemen in the back." It was more of demand than a query. "I know you got to have one of these fresh-today bean pies."

"Not me," the round-faced man called from the table.

"Me neither," the thin man in the felt hat joined in.

The man with the bean pies hung in the doorway for a moment, then ducked back outside with, "I'll have 'em for you next time."

"Muslims is something else," the barber muttered. "They can git pushy, too. But you got to give it to them; they keep their fronts together, keep their hair neat, an they hustle like I ain't seen niggers hustle in a many a year." He paused, sucked at his teeth. "Ever try one of them bean pies?"

"No," he answered and kept his eyes on the man identified as a Black Muslim, who now talked briefly and animatedly with two nattily dressed men carrying pale pink pie boxes.

"I bet they make a fortune off of them pies," the barber mused aloud. "I might try one someday, you know. Might be good."

"Yeah," he mumbled, remembering the Black Muslims of the '60s, proud, aggressive, even arrogant in their blackness redefined, which restored the black race to historical prominence. In those days "black" meant more than color; it was a state of mind, a condition that impacted on and emanated from the heart and the soul, a beacon—symbolic of a bright new world view founded in the imperative

"I'm Black and I'm proud!"—which was hurled like a war cry, an expletive, into the face of western tradition. And in those days, his pre-Limbo days, the Black Muslims hawked their newspapers like angry evangelists peddling the pages of a great new Black Bible, *the* Bible, which found a great pleasure in berating western traditions, history, and morals, while accepting a darkened version of capitalism. From angry rhetoric to peddling bean pies, *fresh today, gentlemen;* what had happened to the fire in the Black Muslim soul?

"Black Muslims sure have changed over the last few years," the barber intoned, "ever since the old man died. I remember when the Muslims had everybody scared to mess with them, white folks *and* black folks. You almost had to be prepared to fight some of them if you didn't buy one of their papers. Now, I hear they started to let whites into the Black Muslims."

"Ought to call them the *Polka-dot* Muslims," someone laughed from the domino corner.

The barber shook his head from side to side; his eyes showed his confusion. "Times sure have changed around."

"They may be letting white folks in but they sure got them bad niggers scared to mess with them," came from one of the domino players. "Black Muslims walk through the Gardens like they wearing bulletproof clothes. They go in there at any time of the day or night selling fish and them bean pies by *themselves,* but nobody messes with them either.

They got more nerve than I got. I wouldn't drive through the Gardens in a tank."

"They really be steppin' on, like they marchin'," another player added. "Like they soldiers, all dressed up just alike. But you right, ain't nobody I know fool enough to mess with them."

He left the barbershop and stood in the damp gloom, wondering what the late Malcolm X would think of the new course taken by the Nation of Islam in the West. Would he approve? Or maybe it was simply a ploy to keep the awesome powers of the *white* government off of their backs, for tax purposes or something. The Black Muslims would be sharp enough to protect themselves.

Icy breezes rippled across the nape of his neck, chilled his ears. The brief nap in the barbershop chair left him feeling crumpled and drained of energy, but the drizzling rain against his face refreshed him. He went into the liquor store and bought another bottle of vodka and some cigarettes, and then, remembering the rent payment in his shirt pocket, he avoided the interior of the Gardens and walked along the sidewalk on the perimeter of the projects, buffeted on the one side by the shouts and the music bellowing from the Gardens and on the other by the noise of the traffic whirring by on Imperial Highway.

He was lost in thought. Things had changed; he saw that clearly enough. But he had yet to decide whether they had really changed for the better. Even the Black Muslims had softened their stance. Did it mean that Black Power was only a cry of *wolf?* A shouted bluff that dissolved into a fine mist when confronted? And if that was true, had things really changed? Or had people simply adapted themselves to a system that would not change?

And he felt that *black* was no longer a positive symbol but rather the color of defeat and failure, defining people a long way from "overcoming." Had the black publications, which supposedly kept him abreast of what was happening in the so-called "black" world, failed him, misread the signs of the time, or simply ignored them? Or were places like the Gardens symptomatic of something other than the disintegration of racial progress—read *Negro gains?*

Maybe the poverty, the frustration, the despair, the anger, were all self-inflicted, or the side-effects of mental disorders that had nothing to do with race; though he still felt that they might have *everything* to do with racial perceptions. Was the struggle, the fire, and the blood, the anger and the hatred, all forgotten? Were Americans still ashamed to face or acknowledge the vicious treatment accorded to the ancestors of its darker (though brother) citizens in an undeclared war of genocide, closely rivaled in history only by the atrocities experienced by Jews during the reign of the so-called "Super Race" in Germany over a hundred years later?

The gauntlet of complaints had relocated and was now an angry phalanx before the squat green one-story office building, an outpost at the entrance to the Gardens. The windows and the plate-glass doors were protected by wire mesh screens painted the same color as the building. And in a flower-bordered grassy area near the front entrance to the building stood a flagpole from which the national flag hung limply over a sagging California state flag. It looked very military, he thought, like the stockade on an army base.

The parking lot in front of the office building was a jumble of double-parked cars and a tangle of people on their way to join the crush at the front door of the building. Car doors hung open, and droopy-eyed men slumped and slouched behind steering wheels, impatiently eyeing the entrance to the office.

Beyond the parking lot was 114th Street, one of the few openings into the Gardens proper. Cars lined up on Compton Avenue to make left turns into the projects, and people were on the move in spite of the cold, wet drizzle.

A police car snaked by on Compton Avenue, its occupants slumped low in their seats like the drivers of the low-slung cars that crept along the arteries of the Gardens.

Women, children trailing after them, brushed by him and into the office, cursing to themselves, to their companions, at the flat green building where they would pay their rent. No one smiled; there was little laughter, even among the children who skittered back and forth between the buildings, dressed poorly against the weather.

An old man, his pants drooping in the back, showing the tops of torn underwear, shuffled up, openly drinking from a half-pint bottle of whiskey. At his side sauntered an intense young man who scanned the faces of the people around him like a watchdog eyeing suspicious strangers. A woman stopped the old man with, "Mister Jenkins. How you doin' today?"

The old man stopped, rocked back on the heels of overrun shoes, and squinted at the woman in the faded long coat who had spoken to him. The young man stopped a step behind him, folded his arms across his chest, and took a protective stance.

"Doin' a lot better," said the old man, touching a soiled bandage on the right side of his head. "Don't hurt as much as it did."

"You've got to be careful, Mister Jenkins," the woman said. "You know how bad these kids has got around here. They don't respect family, friends, age, or even color no more. I don't know what's gonna come of the race at this rate."

"I ain't gon' worry over them no more," Mister Jenkins grinned through tobacco-browned teeth. "I got this young man to stay in my apartment with me. He ain't scared of these gang-bangers. He looks out for me now. They ain't gonna keep beating me up every month and taking my money like I'm they personal bank."

"Well, you did the right thing," the woman said. "It's gotten so I'm afraid to come out of the apartment to even hang the wash up to dry, let alone go nowhere. These young'uns will as soon shoot you as talk to you."

"I know what you mean," Mister Jenkins said. "I bought me a gun, but they broke in on me anyway, beat me up, and took it. I guess I'm lucky they didn't kill me with it."

"You praise the Lawd for your health, and watch out for yourself, Mister Jenkins. I'm gonna git on home out of this bad weather. Just hope ain't nobody broke in my little place and took all my things while I been gone."

"You know that don't make no difference," Mister Jenkins said, swilling down a mouthful of whiskey. "They break in on you whether you home or not. They ain't scared of much. *Pohleece* won't even come when you call 'em. Especially if it's after dark."

"Well, you git in out of the weather as soon as you can." The woman clutched tightly to her handbag, found a clear path through the foot traffic, and walked away, her head and eyes constantly moving, checking, evaluating every movement around her.

The bodyguard moved towards the door, opened it for his charge, and then stepped through the doorway behind the old man, blocking the path of two women, who hurled a curse at the bodyguard as he let the door close on them.

Holding the bag containing the bottle of vodka close to his body, he opened the wire-protected door and held it open as women, old and young, all with children in tow, pushed past him and into the building with little more than a curious glare cast his way. He felt stupid standing there holding the door for the less-than-courteous throng, and he imagined himself as a cast-iron black man in red shirt and white jockey pants, a ring for tethering horses fixed permanently in his hand, a wicked leer on its painted face. Finding an opening in the traffic in and out of the building, he scooted by a large woman, who blew cigarette smoke in his face as he passed.

Inside, women shoved and shouldered their way to the counter like a crowd gone mad at a department-store basement sale. Beyond the counter that split the large room in two were glass-enclosed booths where somber-faced men and women reeled under the steady stream of verbal abuse spewed across the counter at anyone who looked like they worked in the office and scrutinized the faces of the tenants who crowded the waiting room.

A large woman rested her upper body on the counter and leaned forward, allowing chocolate mountains to spill from the top of her thin cotton house dress. Without a word she shifted her weight, stuffed the mounds back into her dress, and riveted a thick-shouldered, brown-skinned man in a green uniform with an angry scowl.

"When you gon' fix my damn refrigerator?" the woman spat. "I put in a damn service request last week and ain't nobody been out there yet. How am I gon' feed my kids? And who gon' pay me for all that food that done spoiled? I can't even buy no groceries or nothin' because that thing won't keep nothin' cold."

The brown-skinned man brushed his hand over thinning hair and said in an even tone, "Our man has been out to your apartment. He said you've got to defrost your refrigerator. Other than that there's nothing the matter with it."

"The door to the freeze part won't stay closed, and all my meat is spoiling. How you gon' tell me they ain't nothin' wrong wit' that raggedy piece of shit? Y'all better give me a new one or I'm gon' call downtown."

"Your freezer door won't close because of the ice that has formed," the man in the green uniform explained, swallowing back his irritation. "Your refrigerator needs to be cleaned out and defrosted. *You'll* have to do that."

"We'll see about that," the woman stormed. "We'll jus' see about that. I been living here twenty years and y'all ain't never tried to do right by the tenants. I want to see the *manager.*"

"You'll have to talk to one of the receptionists about that," the man said and started to move away.

"Hey, don't you go nowhere," a gaunt woman with a narrow neck yelled at the top of her voice. "I don't want to have to git in nobody's ass about my damn toilet. It's been stopped up for two days. I want it fixed right damn now!"

"I need my windows put in," another woman yelped. "How I gon' keep my kids from gittin' sick if y'all don't fix them broken windows in my unit?"

The man in the green uniform, his expression bored, shrugged his shoulders and disappeared down the hall at the back of the building.

"They all'a time complaining about gittin' they rent but they lettin' these damn places fall apart."

"We're short handed," a neatly dressed woman with wide brown eyes explained from the opposite side of the counter. "We have only one plumber working today. He'll get to your unit as soon as he can. You'll have to be a little patient."

"When he gon' come by?" the woman asked, then looked down at the diapered baby crying at her side and screamed, "Shut yo' damn mouth! I'm sick of yo' cryin'!"

"He'll be there before four-thirty," the receptionist said calmly, leaning away from the counter, where tenants crowded like crows on a fence. "He's working on a lot of service requests."

"Well, I put mine in yesterday."

"Shit, I put mine in way last month and ain't no damn body even come around to take a *look*. What the hell's the matter wit' y'all lazy bastards?"

A peach-colored man in a short-sleeved shirt came out of one of the offices and approached the counter. He adjusted the knot on his tie and forced a smile as he faced the female phalanx.

"You the man I want to see," the big-breasted woman roared, then pushed another woman out of her way and sidled down the counter so that she might face her new target. "When they gon' fix my damn refrigerator?"

"This is a business office," the man said softly, his voice just above a whisper, and the woman was forced to lean forward across the counter to hear him better. It seemed the closer she leaned, the softer he spoke.

"That damn maintenance supervisor say ain't nothin' wrong with it. But he's a damn liar."

"Yeah, *you the manager,* ain't you? Why don't you manage these damn places like they s'posed to be?"

The manager ignored the interference from the throng and silently, almost solemnly faced the woman before him. "I've discussed your problem with the maintenance supervisor," he said, his jaw set hard, his tone low, authoritative. "Now, what I want *you* to do is go home and defrost *your* refrigerator and then *I'll* personally come out and check it out."

"And what if it still doesn't work?" she asked, relenting somewhat. "What am I s'posed to do about feeding my kids. I can't keep no meat in the house."

"I'm sure you can find someone who will keep your food for you," the manager started, "especially since you say that most of it has already spoiled. You do that, and if it still doesn't work I'll see that you git another one."

"Mine don't even make ice!" a woman charged from the crowd.

"I'll talk to you in your *turn,*" the manager offered firmly and then said to the large woman in

211

front of him, "Call me when you have *defrosted* your refrigerator."

P̲ictures of Limbo tramped through his head, pictures of shuffling figures slipping out of their orbits creating a chain reaction of confusion. But he knew there were no men in crisp white uniforms who would rush out and dispense potent tranquilizers to restore order— or at least submission—and quiet compliance.

Afraid to move, he allowed himself to be pushed and shoved until he gained the counter. A smallish woman with curly hair and piercing eyes came out of one of the glass cubicles on the side of the building that faced the parking lot. She walked slowly to the counter and motioned for a young woman with hard eyes and a loud rasping voice to step up to the counter.

"Mrs. Brown," the young woman rasped, waving her arms wildly, "they ain't put the windows in my…."

Mrs. Brown, the woman from the glass cubicle, narrowed her eyes and said in a commanding yet somehow motherly tone of voice, "Young women don't curse and scream in public. You just moved in here this week and now you're coming in the office like this is some kind of *back street bar.* You must learn to *act* and *speak* like a *lady* if you want someone to help you."

"But they ain't fixed my windows," she whined,

"You said they would fix them."

"I know what I said," Mrs. Brown said, her eyes fixed on the young woman's. "Your windows will get put in as soon as possible. And you've lived in the area long enough to know how hard it is to keep windows in. Now, you go home, and I'll see what I can do to help you. But I don't want you coming in here screaming and hollering like a spoiled brat. You're a young woman with a family to raise. Now you go home and quit causing trouble."

"Everybody else is saying what they want to say," the young woman said sullenly, her eyes slightly downcast.

"I'm not speaking to *everybody* else," Mrs. Brown replied. "I'm speaking to you. Now, if you want to yell and scream, then you go right ahead. But don't expect me to go out of my way to help you."

The young woman looked away, then said sheepishly, "Yes, ma'am."

"Now go home."

"Yes, ma'am."

Mrs. Brown walked back to her office, lit a cigarette, and turned her attention to the woman she had left sitting in her small cubicle. The young woman, cowed now, slipped back through the throng and out of the building.

"Can I help you?" a receptionist asked impatiently, fending off questions and curses like a rabbit dodging chunked rocks.

He took the envelope containing the rent from

his shirt pocket and then placed it on the counter. "Rent," he managed and then started to say something about the leaky faucet in his mother's bathroom but decided against becoming a part of the confusion.

The receptionist took the envelope and dropped it in a wooden box on her desk. "That all?" she asked.

"Thank you," he answered, then elbowed his way through the crowd in the waiting room and out into the cold drizzle, where he felt less cramped, less a member of the chaos though branded as such by his presence in the chaos. And for a wild, exhilarating moment he felt like *running*. "Where?" froze him on the littered sidewalk. *Where?!* Back to the world of Limbo where there was at least structure, predictability no matter how unpleasant? To the South where he knew that though considerable progress had taken place over the years the *Klanwatch* had been reorganized?

Elongated rubbery strides carried him quickly over the debris that seemed now to stick to his shoes, swelling up around his ankles, and he thought of quicksand sucking at his legs like a jello lake gone mad.

Where was the progress? The new day? The new world?

Dark faces undulated around him like specters from a world he didn't know and he walked faster, chilly air stinging tears into his eyes. An old song lyric taunted him:

Nowhere to run to, baaaaby. Nowhere to hide.
Nowhere to run to, baaaaby. No where to hide.

Ahead of him was the reception compound, a deserted rectangular patch of asphalt iced over with crystals of broken glass, where ten basketball backboards rusted in disuse. The outside of the concrete-block gym looked like the inside of a public toilet, violated with graffiti scratched and painted on its walls, identifying something degenerative rather than an assertion of self, of wholeness. To the left of the baseball field, which had been taken over by a population of gophers and was now a pockmarked trash-covered no-man's-land, five boys in black baseball caps casually threw rocks and bottles at the windows of a seemingly vacant apartment. A young girl cradled an oversized portable radio that belched up-tempo chatter backed by driving rhythms. She watched the boys with mild interest, her head rocking to the beat of the music.

Long-faced men huddled under a large tree in an open, parklike area that seemed more a way station to boredom than a patch of serenity. They drank from cans of beer and bottles of wine, angry bloodshot eyes stripping women and pregnant young girls who scurried, wriggled, and sauntered by, clutching purses and handbags to their bosoms, their children hovering under their protective wings. And the hard-eyed men shouted out their manhood to the women, shuffling, stroking the ground with their feet, laughing, jeering, leering, pointing, gesturing obscenely, prancing—disheveled peacocks in a mating dance.

"Hey, sweet mama. Stop a minute. I got something good to lay on you."

"Hey, sweet thing, let me help you spend some of that welfare money. If it wasn't for a nigger like me you wouldn't be gittin' it no damn way."

"Hey, baby. This sweet daddy is game to give you a little time, if you got the dime. Dig what I'm puttin' down?"

"Come here, bitch. Gimme some of that funky stuff. *You know* you want what I got to offer. Come on over here. Have a little taste of this fine wine."

"Shake it, mama. Shake that big ass for me. Do it, mama! Do it for me! Shake it on down. But don't break it on up. I want it in one big piece when I come to take it. Slow down, mama. You walkin' too fast. I want to talk at you."

Most of the women walked on, heads and eyes forward, faces wearing blank expressions, seemingly oblivious to their surroundings. Other stopped, paused to exchange curses, taunts, or joined the men under the tree.

Everyone seemed to be moving—twitching, wriggling, fidgeting, foot-patting, fast-walking, *jammin',* running—caught up in a great whirlpool of sound and activity—energy trapped in downward swirling spirals; and he wanted to lose himself in the confusion splashing around his head, find his own orbit of safety, or—and the thought was the most frightening of all—break free of the gravitational—*traditional?*—pull of the vortex, to soar above and beyond it all or be bashed to pieces in the rapids.

He walked faster, ignoring the chill; raindrops splattered against his face, mixed with salty tears welling up in his eyes, and blurred his vision, softening once hard and frightening edges into willowy shadows that danced and wriggled like the figures in a dream.

Suddenly he needed to urinate. Maybe it was the weather, or more aptly the tension that tattooed the base of his spine with hot needles. He walked faster, flinching at the sound of glass crunching underfoot. And he felt he was a man rushing to nowhere, running to outdistance too much time, which allowed his flotsam-and-jetsam thoughts to be tossed about and against the walls of his mind by his own private whirlpool.

The past had once been a close friend, during those Limbo days when he had to escape his present and was still afraid to look into his uncertain future. Then the past was a warm, shimmering maiden, dancing behind a silky veil. And now, the veil removed, she was maiden turned she-devil; and the past, his past, now present, tore at him with sharpened claws, ripped at his forming dreams, and then, pointing bloodied fingers at the shredded remains, laughed at his naivete, his susceptibility to storytales.

"Let me hold something, *home!*" startled him.

"I'm good for it. You know me! Let me hold something for a few days. You. know how tough things is. Just 'til I git my poor boy."

A thinner, smaller man than he fell into step at his side. He eyed the man from the corners of his eyes; his throat was dry, his spine tingled. He didn't know the man. At least he couldn't remember ever knowing him.

"Come on, brother man, let me *hold* a little something. I know you got a dollar, man. Let me hold a dollar!"

He hurried his steps to the rhythm of the rush of words coming from the thin man. The smaller man matched his pace.

"Hey, brother. What's the hurry? What you runnin' to? Least you can lay fifty, seventy-five cents on me. How that gonna hurt you? Come on, brother."

He pulled his empty right hand from his pocket, flashed it empty palm up, and then jammed it back in his pocket to cover the sound of his jingling change. The brown-bagged bottle of vodka was pressed securely under his left armpit.

"That's awful chilly, brother. Why you want to do me that way? That's a cold way to do a brother, 'specially wit' *Raygun* trying to keep a nigger poor. Why don't you git off of something, you know? A *quarter!* What'd you say, *brother?* A quarter ain't gon' break you. Why don't you up a quarter, *bruuthaaa!?*"

His heart raced, tripped, flipped. He heard and

felt the threat in the little man's voice, and his eyes searched for an escape route that wasn't there.

"Stop a minute, brutha. I want to talk at you a minute. You understand? Let me run a little something past you."

The man's hand was on his right arm. He winced, tugged his arm away, and swallowed back his mounting apprehension and faced the smaller man whose eyes were glazed b.b.s.

"Brother, I don't have any money," he said, a tremor in his voice that sounded strange in his own ears, out of tune with the voices that careened all around him. He cleared his throat, "I don't have no bread, brother."

"Ain't asked you fo' yo' life savings," the little man pressed. "Just a piece of yo' small change, you understand."

"I don't have no money, brother!" he persisted in the lie, knowing, possibly instinctively, that to change his stance would be to invite trouble he did not want, a fight—even death. And he was angry at the little man for *bracing* him so boldly, and at himself for not handling the situation better. "I don't have no money," he insisted. "I just spent my last little money." But he wished he had flipped a quarter—even a dollar—to the little man while in full stride and kept on stepping. But he hadn't, and he felt that he was responsible for forcing the confrontation.

His guilt was short-lived, as loud, angry voices crashed over them and they both turned to see a teenage girl, dressed only in panties, burst from the doorway of an apartment, her breasts flopping like water-filled balloons. She was screaming, and on her heels another woman, dressed in faded jeans and a man's red shirt, ran from the apartment waving a thick leather strap.

"Bitch, bring yo' whorish ass back in here before I run you down and beat you to death!"

"No! No!" the frightened woman yelped, oblivious to her nakedness. "No! Leave me alone. I'll call the pohleece. I'll...I'll kill you if you hit me again."

"Bitch, shut yo' mouth and bring yo' ass back in this apartment. I ain't takin' no mo' of yo' shit. I done too much fo' yo' black ass to take yo' shit *too!*"

"No! Leave me alone!"

"I tol' you what you'd git from me the next time I caught you fuckin' around wit' men. I tol' you. But yo' whorish ass just too hot to listen." She started towards the trembling girl, the strap raised menacingly.

"I'll *kill you!*" screeched the girl, backing away, glass crushing under her bare feet. "Don't come near me. I'm tellin' you I'll tear yo' eyes out."

Dark, curious faces appeared in windows. Doors opened and men, women, and children, some eating and drinking, spilled from the apartments and formed an impromptu audience, inching closer, jockeying among themselves for a better view of the break in monotony.

"Don't make me come after you!" the woman with the strap growled, her voice gruff. "You know what you'll git then." She shook the strap. "Git back in here. Don't make me no madder than I already am."

"She's crazy!" the girl said, turning to the audience. "She's crazy. Somebody do something. Help me."

No one moved. Someone shouted, "Lemme suck on them titties, mama." But no one moved to interfere, to help, to referee.

"You'd better quit fuckin' wit' me and git back in this apartment."

"You're crazy!" she charged.

"Don't make me have to do what I said I would. You know I don't play. I mean what I say." She never took her eyes off of the trembling girl. "I ain't playin'. I'll do what I said I would do."

"You're crazy!" the woman cried, her wide eyes searching the face of her audience for a sympathetic wrinkle.

People watched and listened from a distance; he, like the thin man at his side, did likewise, locked in time and space. A baby cried from somewhere out of sight. Someone laughed.

"I'll fix yo' whorin' ass," the woman in the red shirt yelled. "You think I won't do what I say. But you'll see."

Someone yelled back, "If it was me, I'd kick yo' mannish ass!"

"I'll fix you!" the woman in the red shirt spun

on her heels and raced into the apartment to reappear seconds later, dangling by the feet what appeared to be a chocolate-colored doll.

A baby was bawling somewhere, but the nude girl's shrieks overrode the baby's crying. She flapped her arms like a wounded bird and let out one final screech before dropping to her knees, sobbing convulsively. He knew then what his blurred vision could not detect and started forward on leaden feet. He was in a half-trot when the woman swung the doll-like figure up by the feet and around and around, and he was running now, running, his heart beating near its bursting point, but the cursing woman swung the head of the doll-like figure, now bawling like a real baby, against the side of the pale green and tan concrete-block building with a sickening *splat,* and a bright spray of blood told the tragic story.

A gasp came up from the audience. Someone screamed. Someone laughed. The baby's crying had stopped; still the crazed man/woman slammed the lifeless body against the unyielding building until an icy hush fell over the audience, and only music and the shrill wail of a distant siren clashed about them.

"Awwwwwwww, *shit!"* he splurted, then yanked the bottle of vodka from the bag, broke the seal, and turned it up to his trembling lips. He quickly chased the scorching river in his throat with a second drink and without a word passed the bottle to the little man who now stood stock-still at his side.

The little man took the bottle, "Crazy-ass dyke!" he hissed, drank, grimaced, and drank again, clutching the bottle by its neck. "That's a bitch!" Why didn't somebody *do something?* What the hell was happening to them? Why hadn't he known, *suspected* that it was not a doll? Why hadn't he recognized the signs? His legs tingled, threatened to give way.

The "crazy-ass dyke" tossed the limp, bloody form onto the ground like a broken doll, saying, "That'll fix all y'all's black asses. Never should'a let you keep that nasty, cryin' thing in the first place. Should'a flushed it down the toilet. That'll teach you not to fuck over me!" She brushed her hands together as if cleaning them, then stomped back into the apartment, slamming the door behind her with an angry *bang.*

"Awwwww, shit!" he moaned and wanted to rush into the apartment and beat the "crazy-ass dyke," drag her by the feet screaming from the apartment, and bash her head against the side of the pale green and tan building. But he didn't move. His left hand twitched spasmodically. His right eyelid fluttered. "Awwww, shit!" he said, more loudly, then snatched his bottle back from the smallish man, turned it up to his trembling lips, and drank. Then he screamed out, "Aw, shit!" and drank again before asking of no one, everyone, "Why didn't somebody stop her? Why didn't somebody do something?"

"Why didn't *you* do something?" someone yelled back. "What's holding yo' ass to the ground?"

And then he was angry. How could he have done anything? He was the stranger. He didn't know the way through the maze or its murderous potential. What could he have done *before* it was too late?

"Not me!" he yelled back. "Not me!" And a wave of hot, steamy guilt crashed over him; tears blinded him. "Not me! I've been away. I didn't *know!* How could I have known? Why didn't one of you do something to stop it?"

He stumbled across the glass-littered ground in a daze, his eyes scanning the faces of the people who stood like grave markers, cold, solemn. He stood over the baby's mother, pulled her up with a trembling hand. "Why didn't you say something? Why didn't you let us know what was happening? *Why? Why?*" and he was screaming, his body shaking violently. *"Why? What the hell is the matter with you people?"*

"Nigger who the hell you think you talkin' to?" came from one of the dark faces, he wasn't sure which; tears scalded his cheeks, stung his eyes, and he couldn't see. But he could yell, and he could scream, and he cursed them. *"Damn you! Damn you! What kind of people are you?"*

"Nigger, you best to watch how you talkin'," an angry voice threatened. "You can git yo' ass kicked talkin' bad."

"Why didn't you kick the ass that *murdered* that baby? Why didn't you do something to stop it? Why didn't you save that baby's life?" He shook the girl angrily. "What kind of mother are you?"

"You're hurtin' me," the girl bawled, tried to shrink away, her bare breasts rising, falling, rising, falling. "Let me go! Let me go! You're hurtin' me."

"Someone needs to beat you!" he stormed. *"Someone needs to beat you for what happened!"*

He didn't see the crowd move in around him. He didn't hear their curses, their threats. He could only feel the horror in his soul. A hand was on his arm, tugging, yanking, pulling. A voice filtered through the madness that crashed around him, a familiar voice.

"Let her go! Let her go! You've got to get out of here! Let her go!"

Turning, he stared into Debra Jean's frightened eyes. A smile curled his lips.

"Come on," Debra Jean urged. "Come with me!"

He released his grip on the slobbering, screaming mother of the dead baby and stumbled after Debra Jean, suddenly recognizing that he still held tightly to the neck of the bottle of vodka. He drank. Curses and threats and taunts swarmed around him like angry bees. He turned his head from side to side; the dark faces bobbed and flitted like featureless blobs.

"Don't say anything," he heard Debra Jean say. "Just walk. Hurry. This is no place for you to be acting like that."

"Bet he's on that angel dust," someone charged. "Who he think he is, come talkin' to us like that?"

"Yeah, why didn't *he* do something if something needed doin'?"

"Somebody ought to kick his ass, talkin' all that lame shit, like he's better than somebody else."

"Don't say anything," Debra Jean hissed and yanked at his arm. "Hurry."

"Who's that nigger anyway? Ain't seen him around here before."

"He better take his ass on away from here if he don't want to lose his head."

It was a nursery gone mad. Shrieks, howls, laughter, sobs, curses swooped and dive-bombed, strafed him, and he wanted to explode, become a bomb that would destroy them all, transform the Gardens into an ashy plot.

A door closed somewhere, and the texture of the ground under his feet changed. He blinked away the tears, caught his breath, and saw that he was in an apartment, a duplicate of his mother's, though the furniture was newer.

Debra Jean was talking to him in low, hurried whispers. "What's the matter with you? What were you doing out there? Are you *crazy?*" She stopped as if the word had caught in her throat and was strangling her. He stared into her wide, hurt eyes. "I mean, are you *okay?*"

"I know what you mean!" He found his voice, and it was strangely calm, though harsh from his screaming tantrum. "I'm not *crazy*. At least I wasn't." He sucked air through his mouth and looked away from Debra Jean's liquid eyes, looked for a way out, someplace to hide, to run. "I know what you mean. But you're wrong; I wasn't crazy

226

when I was committed. Wild, yes. Frantic, too. But not crazy. Never anything like that."

"I didn't mean anything," Debra Jean said softly, apologetically. "I...I...."

"It doesn't matter," he offered, close to her, *too close to her,* the odor of her perfume racing up to tickle his nostrils. "I...I've got to face what I was, where I've been; it's a part of me. There's nothing I can do about that."

"You've got to be careful," Debra Jean said. "That's all I meant. *Really.* You've got to be *careful* here in the Gardens. You could have gotten hurt out there."

"But *why?* What's happened around here? What's the matter with people?"

"Black people are just not ready," she spat.

"Black people? What does that mean? *What does it mean?* I'm black, they say. You're black, they say. Would you do that to your child—to anybody's child? No! And I wouldn't either. And I don't know anybody who would...."

Then he remembered his own father, someone he hadn't consciously thought of in years. And he shuddered at the memory of his father, his face rosy hard from drink, his voice slurred—*"Should'a flushed yo' narrow ass down the toilet when I had the chance. You ain't nothing but a liability. No tellin' what I would have goin' for me if I hadn't been saddled with your black ass. You don't look nothing like me no way. Probably ain't even mine. Should'a flushed yo' narrow ass down the toilet when I had the chance."*

"Let me have that," Debra Jean said and took the bottle of vodka from him. "Sit down. I know how you feel."

"But don't you feel anything?" he asked. "Don't you feel horrified?" The words clicked from his throat as he tried to separate himself from the anguish caused by the memory of his father.

"It doesn't do any good to let yourself *feel* what's going on around here. It would tear you apart. Look around you; it's tearing everyone apart. Can't you *see* that? All I can do is try to protect my children until I can get out of here."

"B-but don't y-you want to help?" he was losing control. "Somebody's got to want to do something."

"There's nothing I can do!" she said too loudly, then said more softly, "None of this is my responsibility. It can't be. I've got my own children to raise, my own life to live. I've got to get the hell out of here."

"And g-go w-where?" he managed. "W-where? You can't run. I've tried. I've tried all my life, and they locked me up for it. Maybe everybody is running. But it's no good. It can't be..., it-it can't be. Nothing ever changes."

They faced each other. Tears welled in their eyes, blurred their vision, watered their cheeks.

"I want to be away from here. Someplace where it'll be safe for me and my children. Is that too much to ask? Don't you see?" Tears flowed freely. Her voice faltered. "T-there's nothing here.

Nothing. No hope. Nothing but darkness. No love. Just hate. Everywhere hate, suspicion, treachery. And…and if, if you're not careful, if you're not watching all the damn time, ready to duck, to run, hide, *fight,* the Gardens will kill you. I don't want this for my children. They didn't ask to be born. They deserve more."

"Then what?"

"Then this!"

"Someone has to stay…, to fight this," he fumbled, not knowing what he meant or why he was pressing her so, why he was demanding, even encouraging her to do something he hadn't done. Why should she stay? And he wondered what there was about the place, the Gardens, that rusted the human spirit, its pathways littered with the rusting hulks of wasted humanity, like the castoff war machines that clogged the rutted arteries of remote islands, metal skeletons decaying in the sun.

"W-what are you saying? Fight what? Fight who? *Whom?* The only fight I'm concerned about is keeping food on the table for my children and fighting my way out of here." Her bottom lip trembled; she sucked air through her mouth. "Let the rest of them stay here. Let them rot here if they want to—but not me, and definitely not my children. I'd give them up if I thought I'd have to raise them here until they were old enough to fight their own way out."

"Forget it," he snapped. "I don't know what I'm saying about anything. This whole day has been crazy." He swallowed the word, forced a smile that did not hide his mounting anxiety, a great deal of which was directly attributable to his closeness to her. But he didn't move away. He couldn't. And she, her breasts brushing against his chest, a moist hand on his arm, did not move away. He saw the question in her eyes and said, too quickly, too defensively, "There's nothing the matter with me."

"I...I wasn't...."

"All I did was a little hell-raising where everyone was trying to build heaven. They didn't understand, or if they did, they simply didn't appreciate what I was about." He wanted to say more, tell her exactly what had happened, how he had spent many years evening the score for wrongs done by destroying toilet facilities. He could tell her how he had been betrayed by a woman he had wanted to love, Mary Elizabeth Jackson. But he felt somehow that none of it really mattered. He was the one who had to be able to face his past, his present, and create a future from the confusion of events. And he knew that Debra Jean was not then prepared to listen, to understand, to empathize.

"You don't have to tell me anything," she whispered. "It doesn't matter. It never matters what you were, where you were born, how rich or poor you might have been. All that matters is what you want to be, what you struggle for, what you fight for. Nothing else matters. It can't."

She was crying openly. "No matter how bad things get or what people deny you just because…because…, it's just not fair."

He knew at that moment that she had not gotten the job she had set her sights on. She cried, was about to turn away; he pulled her to him, her head pressed against his chest. He could feel her tears soaking through his shirt, staining his flesh. He held her tightly and a warm rush of hot air swarmed around him. His breathing was clipped, guttural.

"I don't know if it was written to be·fair," he said, feeling a protective glow overtake him. She felt good in his arms, even crying; it made him feel strong, something he had not felt in a great long time. He held her and she looked up at him through moist brown eyes, and he pressed his trembling lips lightly against her forehead, then her tear-stained cheeks, and her lips found his and she wrapped her arms around his neck, pulling his head down toward hers.

He was afire. Her fingers were like hot curling irons on the nape of his neck. Her lips were wet, full, soft, compliant. And he thought of Mary Elizabeth Jackson and the warm nights they had spent tumbling together in sweaty embraces on the levees that flanked Pike's River. His hands fumbled under Debra Jean's leather jacket. His fingers gripped the fabric of her dress. He tugged at the thin material until he felt the warm flesh of her firm thighs. She moved against him and lighted a rigid fire at his groin, and he clumsily pushed his body against hers, forcing them off balance. He held his grip, his fingers digging into the soft flesh of her plump buttocks. And she held fast, her lips now on his neck, her tongue spreading the fire. They slumped to the floor, and he groped blindly to free her breasts and then suckled one then the other, a starved child.

The moment was short-lived. He reached the fiery pinnacle quickly, too early he felt as he lay on top of Debra Jean, her body still moving, bumping, grinding, demanding more than he was prepared to give at the moment. He still felt an accomplishment, secretly promising, even whispering softly into her ear that later it would be better, her promising that there would in fact be a later, another chance, an opportunity for him to rise to a new occasion.

A siren wailed outside, hovered over them, joined by the sounds of other sirens, the shouts of rushing people, the blare of auto horns, and *music,* loud, penetrating, laying out a confused marching cadence no one could follow.

"You'd better go," Debra Jean said, and he stiffened, afraid of being rejected, and she added, "You've got a party being given in your honor. You'd better go. I've got some things to prepare before I can come."

She straightened her clothes, handed him the half-filled vodka bottle, and planted a moist kiss on his lips, her left hand rubbing the length of his now swelling manhood. "Later," she said softly, smiled, kissed him lightly. "Later. After the party, we'll have our own party."

He stumbled backwards from her apartment, then

stared at her now closed door, reorienting himself, feeling electric things he had long ignored. People crashed around him, pushed against him, as they struggled towards the scene of the tragedy. He turned on his heels, shoved at the shoving people, and pushed his way to his mother's apartment, the smell of Debra Jean alive and warm in his nostrils.

FIVE

BREAK OUT THE BOX

The bloody news beat him to his mother's apartment on lips that beat out messages like jungle talking drums.

When he stumbled into the kitchen his mother was listening intently to a neighbor woman who had "seen it all."

"It was that crazy mannish woman," the neighbor was saying. "You know the one. Live over by the baseball field. The one they say married that young girl while she was pregnant by a real man. It was awful; I knew that something bad was going to happen one day behind that arrangement. Everybody knew that just wasn't right."

He could see the pain in his mother's eyes as she took in every word delivered by the stout woman with the dyed red hair. She seemed younger than he, maybe in her middle to late twenties. But he couldn't be sure. There was something about the way she talked, carried herself, the way her eyes went flat and dull, that made it difficult to tell her age. He found the same to be true of the majority of people who lived in the Gardens. They aged more quickly it seemed, physically if not mentally.

"Didn't somebody try to stop it?" his mother asked, then smiled quizzically when he placed the half-filled bottle of vodka on the table and took a glass from the drain board near the sink.

"It happened so fast," the woman said. "So fast." She shook her head slowly from side to side as if it was a heavy weight on her shoulders and if she moved it too fast, too hard, it might roll off onto the floor.

He ignored her eyes, poured a drink into the glass, added an ice cube, and then kissed his mother lightly on the cheek. He was trembling like a whipped puppy and could not conceal it.

"You awright?" his mother asked, her eyes moist. "You don't look well. You should have worn a jacket. Why didn't you wear a jacket?"

Pulling away from her gaze, he fixed her a drink and then sat down in the living room, out of sight but not out of hearing of what was going on in the kitchen. He heard the door push open; someone rushed in out of breath.

"Mama Joyce, did you hear what happened?"

It was a woman. Her voice was shaken, excited.

He didn't detect any pain, any horror, and it bothered him.

He heard his mother. "Mable was just telling me what happened just now." And he heard and felt her pain.

"I was there," Mable said.

"I just come back from over there," the newcomer puffed, out of breath. "It's awful, girl. Blood all on the side of the building. And that baby laying there all...."

"I was *there!*" Mable cut her off. "I saw it happen," she continued. "I was coming from the rent office. And then I heard all this screaming and cursing. But I knew who it was; girl, they always going at it, that young girl and that...that man/woman, that *thang!*"

"I know what you mean. They're always fighting. I don't know why that young girl got herself messed up with that thing in the first place."

"Just weak-minded," Mable said. "Don't you think so, Mama Joyce?"

"I don't know," his mother said softly. "Some people are weak. Some people do things because they think that it's the best thing for them at the time. I don't know. I've seen them together. I've seen them fighting. But I've never really concerned myself about what they did." She paused. "Though I was worried about what would happen when the girl decided to keep the baby. It somehow didn't seem right to bring a baby up in that kind of household."

"That man/woman was thinking about that welfare money," Mable said, matter-of-factly. "That's what kind *she* is. *She* took up with the girl right after the girl got pregnant. Talked her into taking that apartment."

"I hear she chased the baby's daddy away with a gun when he came by to see the baby after it was born."

"It's true," Mable said. "It's true. I *saw* it. I was there, girl. I told Mama Joyce all about it, didn't I?"

"Yes, I think you did," his mother said. "But so much happens in the Gardens. It's almost as if the same thing happens over and over. But I just can't seem to get used to it happening, especially when children are involved. Nothing seems to grow right in the Gardens."

"I blame that young girl," Mable said. "I don't know why she stayed with that *thang* long as she did. I knew that one day that *thang* would kill her."

"B-but the baby...?" his mother started, near tears. "Why the baby?"

"That girl knew that *thang* didn't want her messin' around with no man. She let her keep that baby, and that was the only man she wanted in that apartment. But you know how some of these young girls is."

"She ain't but seventeen," the second woman interjected. "Just *seventeen* and in all this mess."

"She asked for it," Mable smacked, obviously angry at the interference. "She knew how crazy that *thang* is. I heard her tell her that she'd kill her if she caught her talking to any of these half-slick niggers that be hanging around the Gardens. And I've seen her beat that girl's behind like a natural man would do."

"Maybe she didn't believe that she'd do anything to the baby," his mother offered, holding back her tears with mounting difficulty. "Why didn't someone do something before it came to this?"

"Wasn't nothin' nobody could do," Mable explained as if privy to information unavailable to anyone else. "I know. I even tried to talk to the girl, you know. Tell her that she ought to be careful about sneaking around with these men here in the Gardens if she was going to stay in that apartment. Told me that she could do what she wanted to do and that the apartment was in *her* name and couldn't nobody tell her what to do with herself."

"Didn't that *thang* babysit—like it was the daddy or something?" the second woman asked. "I seen her pushing that baby in a stroller going down Compton Avenue."

"You should have seen them when they was all walkin' like they was a for-real family. It was funny, girl. But wasn't nobody crazy enough to say anything when that *thang* was around."

Through the living-room window he could see people rushing by headed in the direction of the tragedy, the spectacle, the *murder.*

"But why did she do that to the baby?" his mother asked. *"Why the baby?"*

241

"*That thang* caught her with the baby's father," Mable said. "The girl brought the baby's father into the apartment thinking that *thang* had gone to work. But that *thang* doubled back and caught them in the bed together."

"But what about the baby's father?" his mother sobbed openly. "Why didn't he stop it from happening? Why didn't he do *something?* He's a man. Why *didn't he stop it?*"

"Too busy tryin' to save his own ass," Mable said. "He ran out of that apartment with his pants in his hands when that *thang* snuck back in and caught them. And he might still be running now. I don't know too many men who want to tangle with that *thang.*"

The crush of people outside had grown to a near mob of anxious sightseers. He gulped down his drink and stared into the empty glass, wanting another, a series of drinks that might help to soften the memory of what he had witnessed. And maybe help him to find an answer to the questions that peppered him like rock salt from a shotgun barrel.

And he thought of the dream he had on the train ride home. The tattered refugees running and the strange ditty:

Git on board, little children,
Git on board, little children,
Git on board, little children.
There's room for many a more.

Shouts and laughter rippled outside the apartment, and he thought of the doll he had seen that morning and he heard its mournful, "Maaaaaaaama," saw its glassy green eyes, its bashed head, and wondered if it was a sign. When he closed his eyes the glass eye was floating on a blood-red sea. He remembered the newspaper article announcing the bloody bludgeoning of fifteen thousand rabbits. And he rocked back and forth, back and forth, back and forth, his clammy fingers intertwined before him. And he wanted to *scream*.

He wanted to scream but was afraid to for fear that no one would understand his pain, understand what sponsored that pain, and why he had to scream or go mad.

Doctors had said that he was afflicted by an obsession with the primal scream, a raw expression rooted in the uncivilized nature that bubbled in his soul out of control. But he had insisted that it was a war cry, a signal to march, the rattle before the strike of the snake, a warning even, given out to avoid much worse, *confrontation*.

In the '60s, before he…before he *ran*—he could accept that now—a fiery young girl, firm of body and black of mind, asked him was he prepared to kill, kill without compunction, without remorse, without anger—as needed. And he had said, "No!" though he had wanted to feel differently, wanted to feel the western macho in his soul that could allow him to kill coldly, with only his own gains in mind.

He had said, "No!" to killing, and when drafted into the army found that killing was taught, encouraged, without remorse—in the name of freedom denied him.

Was it because he couldn't think of killing, at least not then, that his rebellious scream, his revolutionary war cries were misinterpreted? Or had they already degenerated to the level of the absurd, to the level of "felonious" tantrum-throwing in *the first degree?*

Unlike Muhammad Ali, who intimidated his opponents with shouts of *"What's my name?"* when they refused to acknowledge who he had decided to become and then punished them into submissive compliance with stiff left jabs and thundering, mind-bending rights, he could only scream.

He had not learned or developed the power to punctuate his screams, his shouts of defiance, his war cries with force, not necessarily violent but punishing enough or persuasive enough to bring about change.

He had screamed out, but it had taken the years in Limbo to make him recognize that much, much more was needed. But the ones, the prophets, the seers, the voices who could have provided that leadership when sorely needed, were blasted and bludgeoned into eternity.

And they were all dead, properly buried and tearfully mourned. They were all dead, and their names had turned to dust on tongues blowing other games.

When he closed his eyes he heard metallic laughter flapping over him like a great bird, and a voice belched out a monotonous dirge:

Run, niggers, run!
Run, niggers, run!
Run, niggers, run!
There's room for many a more!

Why hadn't he reacted sooner? Why hadn't he rushed over and snatched the baby from the grasp of the *thang* that bashed its life away? Had he been on his own too long and lost his ability to reach out, to extend himself to others? Was that the debilitating side-effect of too great a concern for individual survival—callousness?

Shame, remorse, sorrow, guilt swept over him, but he knew even accepting the responsibility was not enough to cleanse him of the dark scars on his soul that marked his mistakes, his fuck-ups, like the notches on someone else's gun handle.

He saw that the boundaries of his vision had shrunk over the years, like the people of the Gardens, who muscle-flexed in childish fits, tantrums, drunken rages, which confined their movements to the borders of the Gardens.

Sirens were screaming all around, and the rush of people towards the tragedy had not abated. From the kitchen he heard the women talking, rerunning old horror stories.

"Ain't the first time a baby's been killed or hurt, Mama Joyce," Mable said. "Remember that old woman who baked her granddaughter's baby in the oven because she said God told her she had to cook the devil out of the baby?"

"Remember that man that was sleeping with all his six daughters?" another woman added. "Bragged about it too. Even let some of his drunk friends get a little bit."

"I'd kill any man of mine that come puttin' his hands on any one of my babies," Mable threatened. "Niggers ain't nothin' but the lowest kind of dog. Ain't no two ways about that. Especially these niggers that hang around here like a pack of hungry wolves just waiting for a little girl sheep to come their way. They ought to put all they black asses *under* the jail. Shit, don't none of them want to do nothin' but drink and screw. Don't want to help take care of no babies. Don't want to work. Just stand around, talkin' 'bout how good hustlers they think they be. Niggers ain't shit."

"I know what you're talking about. Ain't no good men around. I guess you just got to settle for what you can git nowadays."

"Well, I don't need no man who stands around all the time waiting for the white man to give him something. He got to do better than that if he gonna be a man of mine."

Where were their men?

He wanted to rush into the kitchen and demand to know why they were there—in the Gardens, on welfare, in his mother's kitchen, reliving tragedies as if they were historic moments in time and space.

Were they refugees from the South? Were their parents the ones who ran? Or their grandparents? How many years, generations separated them from their roots? Or were they rootless weeds that lived on the surface of things, moved about by fickle breezes, stationary until another wind moved them on? Where was home for them?

"Mama Joyce, I don't know why you don't try to move out of here," Mable said. "It's bad in the Gardens. They ought to tear this whole place down."

Where would they go? Another project? Another Gardens somewhere, the search for good land a fever in their souls?

Mary Elizabeth Jackson said you could never *escape* home. You could leave home, run away from home, *be* run away from home—but you could never *escape* home. What did she mean? He had thought her parroting of her father's philosophy had been designed to keep her under her father's overly protective wing. But now he wasn't so sure.

Did they see *home* differently? Or was he just beginning to see what home really was?

She had talked of tradition, culture, history; they thrived in Briarville County, she said, even in the chilly, threatening shadow cast by racism. And he knew it to be true. The campus of the historically Negro college across Pike's River from the Quarters was proof of that history, that tradition. A veritable museum of celebrated accomplishments, bronze plaques, classrooms, laboratories, dormitory wings, even the special toilet facilities donated by a wealthy alumnus, bore the names of citizens, albeit second-class in the eyes of some, who had risen above their humble origins, excelled, civilized themselves, and proved themselves to be a credit not only to their own race but too often more importantly a credit and pleasure to that other race that kept them running, achieving, climbing greased poles, though the majority of the Quarters folks and the folks of the backwoods paid little attention to the historic artifacts, more concerned with survival, and their culture, their history, was kept alive in the memories of toothless Amoses who passed the information on whenever someone had the time, or the interest, to listen.

Where were the signs of culture in the Gardens? Where were the plaques, the historical monuments, the signs, the artifacts that marked the passage of strong, purposeful people? Where were the vivid memories of heroic action? If there was no evidence of culture, progress, meaningful tradition—an organic story celebrating life—did that mean it could not be *home?*

Did being born, living, growing up, playing, and dying in a place make that space home? What of family, friends, familiar sites; did their presence make a place home? Or was home more than just *place* and *space?*

"I can't set you free or send you home!" Reverend Nehemiah Pike had told him during his early days in Limbo when he was obsessed with the need to *break out of the box*. "No one can do that for you but you. I can raise an army, and we can storm any jailhouse, beat back the enemy, tear out the bars, rip the walls apart, and build a palace on that spot. But that don't make it home, and that ain't gon' make you *free*. You can say that you free—scream it out from mountains, beat people in the face when they say you ain't—but that don't make you free.

"Folks can write laws that set you free, books that say you free, but none of it means anything when you carry the jailhouse inside you. And that's where they built it, inside you, locking down your soul. That's the jailhouse that keeps you running. It's the one you carry with you. And all the shouting and talking, and legislating and praying, and marching and cursing, and singing and—yeah, even killing and dying—ain't gon' make nobody free until they can tear down the jailhouses they carry around inside themselves.

"You can't outrun it. You can hide it for a while, cover it with new cars and clothes, but you can't *hide* from it. And no amount of medicine or pills, or whiskey or women or money gon' do nothin' more than fool you into thinkin' that it's not there inside you where it's always been. And for a minute you'll jump around like a kid at Christmas, until you wake up and know that it's still there inside you, lockin' down yo' soul."

"When are you free then?" he had asked.

"You free when you decide to *be* free," Reverend

Nehemiah Pike said. "Ain't no other way for it to happen. You free when you walk like you free and talk like you free, and live every day like you free and never doubt that you free, or let anybody tell you that you not free and build that jailhouse around yo' soul. And when you free, you ain't walkin' like nobody else but you. You ain't following behind nobody or leading nobody. But you there to help, because that's part of being free and staying free. When one rabbit can be trapped, ain't no rabbits safe. You remember that. When you free, you got to be naturally free, and that means can't nobody make you be other than what you got a mind to be when you thinkin' right."

Reverend Nehemiah Pike never explained what he meant by "when you thinkin' right," but it didn't matter. At the time he probably wouldn't have understood anyway. Now he felt he did and missed the old preacher all the more because he never had the opportunity to thank him for all he had taught him, though he had made a feeble attempt when he was released from Limbo and climbed the narrow footpath that wriggled through the brush that covered Pike's Mountain to plant a small white cross near the spot where Reverend Nehemiah Pike's Golgotha Baptist Church of the Divine Savior once stood.

And too, though he knew he would never completely agree with Mister Jackson, dean of students at the historically Negro college in Briarville County, he was beginning to see some truth, some insight in the observations Jackson made when he damned the ragged and beaten lines of migrating southerners as refugees, stripping them of any heroic proportions. Maybe they carried their jailhouses with them, though running gave them momentary reprieve from their sentences, allowing them to exchange outhouses and Negro-only washrooms for indoor plumbing, where they could act freely.

Few of them came home, at least not until the struggle ended and victory was announced. Most of them couldn't come home because of the struggle, because they had rooted themselves in concrete-block-and-brick "Gardens" throughout the country and were wallowing in newfound freedoms they could not take home with them, not until victory day, until freedom was hacked into the granite face of racism by those who remained to struggle, never looking north or east or west or over Jordan for anything but support. They needed no asylum.

And when the battle dust cleared, swept away by a truce scripted by white fathers, black magazines and newspapers trumpeted the end of struggle, heralded and celebrated the dawning of a New Day in the South, some say too soon. But the refugees, those who could afford to, straggled back to the South, to home, where life was much simpler, they felt, than that new land across the river and beyond the great Cotton Curtain. They straggled back, not as they had left, shaking the dust of the South from their running feet but haughty, sophisticated, urbanized, sporting bright and shiny souvenirs of their exile in the "promised land."

The black press had wooed them from the South with promises of freedom, wealth, hope. And it was the black press who castigated them for their lack of etiquette, for their slowness to conform to the urban way, and damned them for their own continuing victimization, holding a plastic so-called "black upper-class" as examples of what the best of the race could do, as proof that *all* niggers weren't inferior.

And it was also the black press, at the bidding of mercenaries in three-piece suits who had replaced the warriors who had led the struggle that routinely threatened the majority populace with "long hot summers," during which the refugees who could not return south, who did not succeed outside the South, restricted to government-financed reservations passing as low-income progress, would no longer be able to suppress the anger, hopelessness, poverty boiling in their souls, and would spill violence from their souls like a river gone mad.

None of it had changed anything. The promise of long hot summers had long since lost its threat, falling into the category of crying wolf.

He knew that he couldn't run again. Not then, even though he saw that the struggle was far from over, that the battle lines would have to be redrawn and remanned. And he was afraid, afraid because he knew what lay ahead of him, of all of them. And he wanted to scream out the apathy that hobbled him, scream it out of his system so that he might be able to make decisive moves, *freely*. He needed to scream out and shatter the cocoon that entrapped him. He had been released, yes, but he was not yet free, he was not yet home, he wasn't yet *home free*.

There was activity in the kitchen. The smell of food was sickening him. He heard new voices.

"Mable, television cameras are all over the place," someone who had just come into the apartment said in a hurried voice. "Channel seven, channel four, channel two, all of them. Saw the trucks myself. And you know that cute announcer with the curly hair, he's out there asking everybody questions about what happened."

"You kidding, girl," Mable said. "Who they asking?"

"They asking everybody who want to git on television and say something. I'd a said something to him myself but I didn't see nothin'. I was to the store cashing my check I sure wish I had been there."

"Girl, *I* was there!" Mable exploded. "Ain't that right Mama Joyce?"

"Yes," his mother said weakly. "Mable has told me that she saw the whole thing."

"Mable, if I was you and seen what you seen, I'd be right there talkin' to that cute announcer. I'd tell him everything he want to know, and a few things that I got on my mind."

"I know what you got on yo' mind," Mable laughed. "But it ain't nothin' he gon' want to hear. But you right, I ought to go down there, you know,

tell them what I seen. Ain't nobody know them people no better than me."

"They already done took that *she-he* away in the
pohleece car. She didn't say nothin'. Just went
along with them like they was gon' take her for a
ride in the park."

"That *thang* is crazy," Mable said. "I'm gonna
go on over there, Mama Joyce. I'll come back and
help with the party when I'm through."

"You take your time," he heard his mother say.
"I can handle everything."

He felt sick, nauseous, as if his whole system
was forcing its way up through his throat. His body
convulsed. He flushed hot, then cold, then scorching hot. His fingers trembled, his eyes watered. His
legs were the spastic limbs of a black-faced buck-
'n'-wing dancer, tattooing out a chaotic, frenzied
rhythm on the tile floor. He heard movement; someone left, and now someone—his mother?—was
walking towards the living room. He bolted up from
the sofa and raced for the stairs. His foot missed
the first step and he fell forward, slamming his head
into a wooden step. Panic-stricken, he clawed at the
steps with his hands and feet and managed to scram-
ble to the top of the stairs and into the small bathroom without being seen. And once there he knelt
over the porcelain throne and pitched up his breakfast. His throat was raw, his stomach a mass of pain.
When the spell passed he weakly splashed his face
with cold water, then stared at his reflection in the
mirror.

He had stopped running, shuffling, orbiting in tight, tiny circles. He knew that it had to be over if he would ever be free of what had been assigned to him, defeatist tags that were designed to keep him *hop-hop-hopping, skittering,* and *scooting, ducking* and *dodging. This* nigger-rabbit wasn't running anymore. He had found his space, and he was going to make it worth calling home. But for the life of him he wasn't sure how. Still, he knew, and it was a great step forward for him, he knew that it wasn't simply a case of black against white, negro-only toilets *vs* white-only toilets. It was about freedom, the freedom to construct his future himself out of all the cultural artifacts left by the cultures of man, as *he* so chose. He was not an escapee, no longer a runner before the gun, a dreamer. He was no longer refugee, though he had dragged his tail home hoping that he could feast at the table of freedom in exchange for all the dues he had paid thus far.

But he was dreaming even then. He had not earned the feast. The feast itself was premature, and now that he recognized that, he felt that he could survive and that he was prepared to struggle, but first he had to rid himself of dead dreams, and he screamed out—"Aaaaaaaaaaarrrrrrggghhhhh," to the walls of the porcelain cell and felt the reverberations trembling his body. He was ready to fight. He had issued his last warning!

A souvenir child, he was a silent shadow on the streets, shouting his manhood in dark crevices

between sizzling thighs, bent on perpetuating himself in Kewpie-doll micro-shadows on the streets,
until they grew to become like him, running, a silent
shadow on the streets—or they might stop and
scream and fight, souvenir child running wild!